The Last Saxophone

A Story About The Soul Fathers

Thos Judge

www.thosjudge.com

Copyright © 2019 Thos Judge

Paper Back Edition

All rights reserved. This book or any portion thereof may not be reproduced or used in any manner whatsoever without the express written permission of the publisher except for the use of brief quotations in a book review or scholarly journal.

ISBN: 978-1-0974-0142-0

Any resemblance to real persons, living or dead, or real places or events is purely coincidental. This is a work of fiction. Any names or characters, businesses or places, events or incidents, are fictitious. Any resemblance to actual persons, living or dead, or actual events is purely coincidental.

Artwork by Ian Aspinal

www.thosjudge.com

PRELUDE

If a man loves a woman but cannot have her, then the best thing that he can do is to invent a world where they can be together.

If he can write this into a story they can be together forever.

To Bob, thanks for the inspiration.

CONTENTS

1	On Campus	1
2	Karaoke Land	6
3	Penitentiary Psychiatric Hospital	10
4	Escape	15
5	Journey Across Tenerife	21
6	Living In Las Americas	29
7	Everyday People	37
8	At The Hard Luck Café	41
9	Joy Casino Del Sur	47
10	The In Crowd	52
11	The Soul Wagon	57
12	Building A Community	61
13	Confession	66
14	The Ultimatum	71
15	Cry For Help	76
16	Looking For Lorenzo	83
17	Trial	86
18	Recovering Lorenzo	92
19	Back At The Pesto Restaurant	96
20	Band Meeting	101

21	Accident Waiting To Happen	107
22	Kissing My Love	112
23	Brief Return To The Future	116
24	Return To The Future	122
25	Second Coming	126
26	Living In The Past	133
27	The Benefit Gig	139
28	Leaving Tenerife In A Hurry	144

1 ON CAMPUS

I am #TMp319, we don't have names here, we have hash-tags. Names were abandoned many generations ago, as they were considered too egotistical. I'm studying Soul Music here on Campus. My other role in life is as a hydroponics engineer, which I am told is a worthwhile profession and essential to the community and not my choice unfortunately.

I was quite surprised to be congratulated by Prof. #ELv15 as he never congratulated anybody. He had told all the other students that I was a role model and an exemplary musician. My prize was to be shown around the museum and I couldn't wait.

The deputy of the museum, #ELv151 took me by the hand and we walked through those hallowed gates. I hadn't anticipated smashing his head in later, with Jimi Hendrix's guitar. It was the furthest thing from my mind. This is a museum of musical instruments you see. The rumours were that Prof. #ELv15 had been secretly performing Karaoke somewhere and he had access to a time portal so that he could go back to the Twenty First Century. It's a bit far fetched I know, but that was the gossip on the Campus. None of the other students had been inside the museum but they all knew what was there.

As soon as I saw the golden saxophone I had to play it. I

wanted to put the alligator skin strap round my neck and blow on the golden mouthpiece. It is claimed that the sax had once belonged to a President of the U.S.A. wherever that was. These old countries are no more, and I'm just not interested in political history. I am a student of musical history, soul music to be precise and with a specialism in James Brown. Yes I know Soul Music has a political angle to it because it is black mans' music and the music industry was the realm of the white man, but actually I'm only interested in the music not the politics.

When we arrived beside the old gold saxophone I reached out to the instrument but #ELv151 blocked the way.

"Don't touch anything," #ELv151 whispered telepathically.

Now I know very well that sounds are forbidden in this world, but I just wanted to pick it up. I know I can play it because I had been learning lots of instruments in the simulator and so I was confident that I could get a tune out of it.

Jimi's guitar was next to it on a stand and I had the sudden urge to pick up the guitar and smash the deputy's head in. I collected my thoughts. Once the deed was done what would I do next? Toot a tune on the sax then leave the building gracefully? I knew that I couldn't live in the museum forever with the decomposing corpse of #ELv151.

We wandered around the exhibits, past Billy Cobham's drum kit and Gene Krupa's kit too. There were lots of drum kits and a cornucopia of other instruments but only one saxophone. This is allegedly the last saxophone in existence. It was just begging to be played.

"Sir, does anybody ever play these instruments?" I asked.

"Officially no. But unofficially yes. It's a perk of the job," he answered.

"Who gets to play the sax?"

"It's the only one that nobody plays. Nobody can get a sound out of it."

I pondered the silent reply and wandered over to peer at Louis Armstrong's trumpet.

"Don't touch."

I knew not to touch anything and Satchmo's trumpet did not attract me like the golden sax did. It was gleaming at me from across the room. The instruments had been acquired over hundreds of years. After the great European Sound Directive of 2230, which stopped all but personal music through headphones, no more musical instruments had been made. Except of course those that could be heard only with headphones. Thus the world became silent of loud music at that point.

The museum was quiet but suddenly there was a low hum for a few seconds and then a door opened with a whoosh and out stepped Prof. #ELv15 in his full Karaoke costume, complete with blue-black quiff on his head and shades on his long nose. He marched past with his diamante cape flowing behind. I guessed the room he had come from was where the time portal was situated.

Rory Gallagher's battered old Stratocaster looked appealing but not fit for my purpose. I couldn't see anything belonging to Pete Townsend. One of his guitars would have been quite apt though.

If only the deputy would let me pick up the sax and let me play it then I wouldn't need to do this deed. I did my best not to kill him, just to knock him out.

A few moments later I found myself with the gold sax slung around my neck on the alligator skin strap, standing in the chamber that Prof. #ELv15 had left a few minutes before. I couldn't imagine killing an animal for its skin, although I had heard that back in the Twenty First Century people ate alligators and that the meat tasted like chicken. I'd never tasted chicken or alligator for that matter although I have seen images of chickens. I can't imagine what the flesh of a dead animal might taste like. How barbaric they were back then. But now in this world we don't have any animals at all because they are no longer needed. Someone told had told me that their DNA was preserved somewhere just in case the human race needed to grow more of them. I'd also heard about other barbaric practices from back then. It made my stomach turn to think that baby humans were grown inside a woman's body.

Thankfully I thought that we are all now manufactured normally in a more humane way without using another person as a host. I thought that it would have killed the host and I also remembered that some women were forced to lactate in order to feed their babies. And of course once the baby was old enough it was forced to eat the flesh of a dead animal. It's frightening to even think of this. And as for death, nobody knew when he or she was going to die. People in the past lived daily with the expectation that some illness would kill them eventually. There was no certainty to life or death back then.

Once the scientists had got all the diseases under control it was obvious that the planet could not support a population that didn't die. The answer was to engineer new-borns to have a specific expiry date. I am gifted with dropDead@40.gene. This is now the norm for all males and we are blessed with seven years of freedom before we finally pass away because females are all fitted with dropDead@33.gene. So much for equality and there were many pressing for both sexes to have dropDead@33.gene. But of course all are at the mercy of the World Controller.

The wall panel showed 3 Sep 2019 in red and I guessed that was the last date that Prof. #ELv15 had set for his previous foray into Karaoke Land. I pushed down hard on the big green button below the panel. The low electrical hum that I had heard before started up again only a little louder. I could feel the room descend for a few seconds and then it stopped, as did the noise.

THE LAST SAXOPHONE

The door on the other side of the small room slid open and bright sunlight lit up the space around me.

   I stood apprehensively holding the gold saxophone to see what would happen next.

2 KARAOKE LAND

Music: Call Me Super Bad – James Brown

The smells of Karaoke Land drifting in were different to those of the Campus and so I took a big gulp of air from inside the room and leant out of the doorway into the sunshine. It was incredibly hot and I could see the sky and guessed those white things must be clouds. And the bright thing must be the Sun.

I could feel my heart pound excitedly in my chest and reasoned that if Prof #ELv15 could do this then so could I. And so I stepped out into the brave new world of Karaoke Land and stood absorbing the scenery. This must be what outside looks like? I've never been outside before, it's not allowed.

I looked around to get a reference point so that I could find the portal again later. I could see that it had opened up at the base of a stepped pyramid and so I counted the number of rocks either end of the pyramid to the center of the portal entrance. The pyramid had a flat top and was very tall and quite similar to others standing nearby.

I felt good and could hear the sound of James Brown the Godfather of Soul in my head but strangely different. Normally when I thought of a tune, it played in my head. The Network probably wasn't working here or the signal from Campus wasn't strong enough to reach me. Maybe it's got something to do with being in the past? This is it quite worrying because my other apps probably won't work either.

    I stood and adjusted my orange hemp suit and realized that the environmental management system wasn't working. Venturing across the brown ground I recognized that those things on the surface must be wild plants growing there. I didn't have access to the database to find out which ones they were. I stopped to look closer but the sax was quite heavy and I soon regretted not leaving it in the time portal. Maybe there was an opportunity to be a Karaoke saxophonist in Karaoke Land?

    I decided to play the sax to make sure I could get a tune out of it. It was very easy to play and the gorgeous sound drifted upwards towards the sunshine and clouds. As I walked further away from the pyramid the ground became smooth and black and suddenly the noise increased and a massive machine came thundering by. I jumped back onto the brown ground to avoid being hit and the giant machine made an angry noise as it went past.

    The black ground was obviously dangerous as next several motorcycles went past. I recognized these from the simulator training I had done. I think the big noisy machine was a truck if I recall correctly. It's used to transport goods, such as bits of dead animals for people to eat.

    The heat felt good but I was starting to perspire and my orange clothes were getting damp. Being alone was a little scary at first but I needed to keep walking as I could see the sea in the distance. I'd never seen the sea before except in images and was curious to find out if it really was wet like drinking water. I was also getting a little thirsty. Where could I get a sip of water?

    A machine stopped but the operator spoke to me in a

language I didn't understand and so I ignored it and kept on walking with the sun shining behind me. After a while I had to negotiate a massive construction that allowed the machines to change direction. To avoid injury I used the steps to climb around it and eventually I got back on the route taking me in the direction of the beautiful azure sea.

Finally there were buildings and many people and as I got closer to the sea I could feel the coolness of the breeze. It was very noisy and I was now starting to wish that I had never left the Campus. As I stood in the shadow of a large building I collected my thoughts and decided to have another blow on the saxophone.

Many people came to stare at me. Maybe they were listening to my playing or maybe they thought I looked strange. Everybody else was so small and most of the men had really short hair.

A blue machine stopped and the two short fat men in blue and black clothes inside it are watching me play. People have put small pieces of circular metal in front of me. Maybe it is an offering because I am aware that most people in the Twenty First Century still believe in one of many Gods. But the two men in the machine just stare. Maybe they do not believe in God because they have not made an offering.

One of the men in the machine shouts but I cannot hear him clearly. So I stop playing and he shouted again but I could not understand his language. I guess they like my playing. This encouraged me to play some more for them.

The two men get out of the machine and approach. One of them seems very agitated and his voice has an edge of fear to it but I ignore him. If I play some more it will pacify him I am sure.

The man comes so close to my face that I can smell his appetite but he needs to look up because he is much smaller than me. He isn't very happy about something and so I stop playing.

The calmer of the two men pulls at the sleeve of my orange suit. He also speaks in a language that I do not understand.

"Boom bi di boom, boom bi di boom. Dear friends how may I be assisting you?" I think I have used my voice for the first time ever.

The angry one takes out a book of paper and a writing implement. I recognize these from images I have seen. They do not seem to understand me and so I repeat the phrase but much slower.

The calmer one walks behind me and pulls my hands behind me and locks them together with a device.

I am walked forcibly to the machine where I am pushed inside. The one who is not controlling the machine has taken the saxophone and is sitting holding it in the front seat of the machine.

The machine moves off with me inside. I am being taken somewhere new. I hope there is Karaoke there because this is the purpose of my trip.

3 PENITENTIARY PSYCHIATRIC HOSPITAL

Music: Sexual Healing – Marvin Gaye

"Hey sister, who's the new guy?" Lorenzo asked the gorgeous nurse as he nodded in the direction of the tall thin man with the dreadlocks.

Sister Martina was the prettiest nurse he'd ever seen and her blond hair hung in escaped random wisps from beneath her white coronet, which contrasted with her black habit. She was easily distinguishable from the other sisters by her stunning shapely figure. Lorenzo continued to mop the floor bashfully. This was part of his duties in the psychiatric ward attached to the penitentiary.

"I don't know, Lorenzo. He keeps telling us he has no name just a hash-tag."

She then informed Lorenzo with her Czech accent that the inmate he had nodded towards had no papers and did not speak Spanish. He had been arrested for illegal busking but had claimed he had come from the future and this was why they had put him in the psychiatric wing. The papers authorizing his detention referred to him as Mr. Saxophone.

Lorenzo looked up from the floor straight into her beautiful clear blue eyes.

"What are you in for man?" he asked in English with his back turned to Mr. Saxophone.

"Boom bi di boom, boom bi di boom. I da sax man an' a play what I can," he replied in a weird accent. It sounded sort of Jamaican to Lorenzo and he spoke in rap lyrics.

Lorenzo guessed that Mr. Saxophone didn't know what he was in the psychiatric ward of the prison hospital for and continued to mop the floor. It's part of the duties he volunteered for. Being a prison inmate is tedious and you need to find things to do to help pass the time.

"I was told you were busking illegally."

"Busk bi di busk, boosh bi di busk? What's dat?" he replied.

"Playing a musical instrument in public without a license."

He grunted and made a few noises. It was obvious that he didn't understand the reasons behind his arrest. Lorenzo learned from him that he played many instruments but had been playing a golden saxophone at the time of his arrest.

"You know you're in Tenerife don't you?"

"No mon, I am in Karaoke Land. Boom bi di boom. The professor comes here to perform, he is a storm and is got da form."

His reply made no sense and so Lorenzo asked him what his name was?

"I am #TMp319 mon," he answered.

"Your name Tom Perignon is it?" That's what it sounded like to Lorenzo.

"Call me what you want. I am who you want me to be. Where I come from we don't have no names. What you get is what you see. Boom bi di boom."

"So where are you from then?"

He kept his head down as he mopped the floor but he was also aware that sister Martina was listening in on the conversation too. She obviously understood English although they had only ever conversed in Spanish. Lorenzo thought she was an interesting lady as he had heard that she had been an Olympic sword-fencing champion and an acrobat. He guessed this is obviously how she kept her trim figure. He also guessed she was about 30 years old but not sure whether she was single or had kids. All he knew was that she flirted at him with her lovely blue eyes that were like a sky sown with stars and with a perfect pouting mouth full of gleaming shiny white teeth. Lorenzo could also see the yearning in Tom Perignon's eyes as he foolishly eyed sister Martina's body.

Lorenzo distracted him from his lust by asking him the question again and this time he elicited a response.

"I am a man who come here in a van. People take me as fast as they can. Boom bi di boom, boom bi di boom. It's easier for me to explain that I am insane and I come from a future time where everything's just fine."

"A future time. What do you mean six o'clock?"

Tom turned to stare at Lorenzo angrily. "No mon, several hundred years or maybe thousands of years in your future. Where we are not barbarians." Tom had a moment of rapless speech and he placed a particular emphasis on the last sentence.

"Really," Lorenzo replied dubiously. But it actually did seem like the truth however implausible that might be. Clearly the local magistrates had thought otherwise and had him locked up for his own safety.

"Why do you say we are barbarians?" Lorenzo asked curiously.

Lorenzo learned from his new friend that many things in his alleged future were different. Most importantly nobody eats the flesh of animals and that it is a silent tomorrow-land populated by motherless manufactured clones.

Obviously Lorenzo had his duties to attend to and so he made a point of returning every day to learn more and of course to flirt with sister Martina.

Over the next few days he discovered that Tom was a music teacher and specialized in Soul Music from the Twentieth and Twenty-First Centuries. Tom was also a hydroponics engineer and with the help of the ever-willing sister Martina they got him a little work in the hospital garden and also had his saxophone returned. After all he wasn't accused of theft and so the gold sax was his personal property.

One day as Lorenzo was mopping the toilets he found Tom writhing in agony on the floor. The spasms continued for some four of five minutes and then he lay motionless and breathing heavily. Lorenzo could swear he had been clean-shaven earlier but now Tom had a full beard.

Not being a medically trained professional all he could do was to stand leaning on his mop watching Tom's contortions. Eventually Tom opened his eyes and gave Lorenzo a glazed look.

"You ok?"

Tom sat up and answered in the affirmative.

"What's up with you?"

"Not know. Never happen before. Boom bi di boom."

"You look a little different. Your beard, did you have that earlier? It's about three months growth. You didn't have it yesterday did you?"

Tom felt his face for several minutes then pulled his long skinny frame up slowly and looked in the mirror above the hand-drier and muttered something under his breath as he brushed his long blond dreadlocks away from his face.

When Lorenzo saw him the next day he was clean-shaven again and was chatting in English to Martina. Lorenzo mopped his way towards them slowly and gracefully.

"How you feeling today Tom Perignon?"

"Who is Tom Perignon?"

"You are, my friend. I think it suits you."

"Yeah call me what you like. I can be Tom Perignon for you and everybody else if you say so. But I am not a substitute."

He seemed embarrassed and told Lorenzo that he was going out to work in the garden. Tom had made some very significant improvements there and it was evidence that he had superior knowledge of hydroponics as he had erected some vertical growing pipes, which appeared to have plenty of growth on them. Lorenzo mused how good he might be with Satan's spinach, which was Lorenzo pet name for Ganja.

"Can I hear you play a little tune on the sax?"

"Maybe later. Little later. You come?"

Lorenzo only worked morning duties in the hospital wing and so had to be back in his own ward by two pm. Lorenzo had previously spent several months in the psychiatric ward and was now assessed only as borderline crazy. The primary reason he had volunteered for duties there was so he could meet with sister Martina because a man needs to live in hope even though she is about fifteen years younger than he was. And so Lorenzo would find a way to be there later for sure.

4 ESCAPE

Music: Papa Was A Rolling Stone - Temptations

The hospital was part of an old monastery and the Poor Fathers of Tenerife came to visit the penitents in the late afternoon and early evening and so Lorenzo hatched a plan.

The fire alarms were ringing when he walked into the ward dressed as a priest. Sister Martina seemed unsurprised by his holier than thou appearance.

Lorenzo took Tom by the hand outside onto the terrace and handed him a bundle of clothes.

"You want hear me play? Boom bi di boom. I don't know what to say. So I use my saxophone every day."

"I've heard you play. I'm in the other ward. Put these on and grab your sax," Lorenzo ordered. "And can you please stop speaking in rap lyrics."

Tom gave him a blank look.

"Holy guacamole, put the clothes on and come with me. We are getting out of here. This is a lunatic asylum. We are perfectly normal."

"Where are you two going?" asked Martina as she laughed at both of them in their costumes.

"We are getting the hell out of here. That's where we are going." Lorenzo answered in disbelief. He didn't think she'd be so casual about their escape plans. Also he didn't think she would want to come with them so he didn't bother to ask.

She muttered something in what he assumed to be Czech and then took Tom into the bathroom and clipped off his dreadlocks whilst Lorenzo set fire to his bed. Now Tom looked more like a priest. There are not many priests with dreadlocks and they tend to stand out in a crowd. And of course his bed was now burning. It must have been an act of God.

The three of them shepherded the other patients of the ward out into the late afternoon sunshine and they mingled with all the doctors, nurses, patients, psychiatrists and priests whilst they waited for the fire brigade to arrive and extinguish the several small blazes that had occurred in their path.

Lorenzo took Tom by the arm to the gate and as soon as they opened it the fire engine came through. They walked out only looking conspicuous because Tom was carrying his golden saxophone hanging from his neck on an alligator skin strap.

"What you name?" Tom asked.

Lorenzo had never thought to tell him and he'd never asked before. He introduced himself as Lorenzo Pitiful, which is almost his name.

"You from this place?"

Tom was becoming inquisitive and Lorenzo hoped that this

was a good thing. He explained about his Italian heritage but that he had been living in Ireland for a while. This was meaningless to Tom as his knowledge of geography was non-existent.

They stood outside the monastery gates in the evening twilight. Lorenzo knew they had to act quickly to get away from the penitentiary before they could draw too much attention to themselves. Lorenzo didn't want to steal a car, as that would cause further complications especially if the police stopped them.

"Why so many small people?" Tom asked.

"Small people? Where?"

He pointed at the children walking with their parents. Lorenzo informed him that these were children. This was a concept Tom didn't understand at all and clearly there were no children in his Tomorrow Land of motherless beings.

Tom explained that clones were manufactured in a processing plant or a maturing facility as he called it. Once the clone was hydroponically grown to adulthood they were born or hatched to use his terminology. Although Tom was twenty-one years old he had only been hatched three years ago. Three years ago in the future that is.

And then Tom hit Lorenzo with the big one. "I need to go to the bathroom."

"Holy guacamole," Lorenzo replied in shock.

"I got brown shoes and I need number twos."

It seemed that the boy from the future had special dietary requirements and his digestive system could not handle the food he'd been eating.

They ran across the road with their cassocks billowing and entered Gigi's a small Italian restaurant. Lorenzo pointed him in the direction of the bathrooms at the back. He'd been there before in some of his previous escape attempts. Lorenzo took a seat away from the window and called the waiter in Italian and ordered two plates of spaghetti with pesto and two glasses of red wine. Everything was homemade and Lorenzo was addicted to pesto, the green one made from fresh basil.

Tom returned looking refreshed and Lorenzo invited him to sit down and explained that before they would do anything they would eat some good food. The world was always a better place on a full belly of nice food. Lorenzo knew this to be a material fact.

Tom sat staring at the walls of the restaurant where there were mounted two tenor saxophones and an alto. He rested his gold tenor on his lap. Luigi the restaurant owner came over and asked to see the sax but Tom would not let it go.

"Father Tom is rather attached to his instrument."

"You should keep it in its case Father. It will get damaged otherwise. It's a very fine instrument. Is it solid gold?" asked Luigi.

Lorenzo answered in the affirmative, as Tom did not understand Italian. Luigi went to the store-cupboard and returned with a brown leather tenor saxophone case and offered it to Tom. Lorenzo helped him dismantle the sax and put it in the case observing that Tom seemed unaware of how to do this.

Lorenzo thanked Luigi and offered to sing him a song. He'd done this before when he'd escaped from across the street. Normally he went straight back to the hospital after a good meal and a song or three.

Luigi's favourites were 'That's Amore' and 'New York New York', his favourite singers being Dean Martin and Frank Sinatra. Lorenzo guessed that Luigi thought he really was a Poor Father of Tenerife because he never charged him anything for the food and drink. Lorenzo's other job at the hospital was working in the laundry and he always had access to a supply of clean clothing.

Two plates of steaming food were placed in front of them and Tom eyed them quizzically. After Lorenzo had explained that there were no bits of dead animal used in the making of the meal Tom sampled it and then ate rapidly. After an explanation and two sips Tom gulped the wine down and asked for more.

"I like this wine it has a good affect on my head."

"Be careful, we need to be able to walk," Lorenzo advised him. For a few days Lorenzo had not entirely been convinced that Tom was really from the future. But Tom's lack of understanding of so many things was an enigma and evidence that there was some truth in his story.

"Do you like beer?" Lorenzo asked him. He had to explain what beer was.

"Where are we going and what are we going to do?" Tom demanded.

"Listen, with your sax playing and my singing we are going to the other side of the island and we are going to make it big on the music circuit there."

"Karaoke Land yes I want go there and play. But need go back say goodbye to Martina. And also my garden, me want bring plants. Me like tomatoes."

"Tomatoes? Why tomatoes?"

It would seem that in the future world there are no tomatoes and all the fruit and vegetables that are grown are different. It clearly was a strangely different world.

"We don't have time for any of that. As of now we are gonna be The Soul Fathers and we are on a mission to save the world from shit music."

Luigi had a second job in a big five-star hotel in Los Gigantes on the west of the island and offered to take them there when he closed the restaurant. This was a good move that would get them far away from the penitentiary.

5 JOURNEY ACROSS TENERIFE

Music: Thank You For Taking Me To Africa – Sly & the Family Stone

They wandered through the huge hotel lobby wearing their cassocks and with Tom carrying his sax in the new case.

Lorenzo asked at reception for the entertainments manager and told him that they were the evening's entertainment and that the agency was substituting them for another act. They were directed to the open-air stage near the pool and invited to eat in the restaurant. The views to sea were stupendous and the moon had yet to rise but the lights on the island of La Gomera opposite could be seen winking at them across the water.

Wandering through the restaurant shouting 'Hallelujah' because they are The Soul Fathers they blessed everyone they saw. They availed themselves of the catering facilities and gorged on bowls of ice cream. Unfortunately there was no pasta and pesto on the menu and Tom was disappointed that they were not allowed to drink wine.

Lorenzo plugged his phone into the sound system to use his backing tracks and Tom assembled his sax. They needed to start the show before the scheduled act arrived. Once they were playing nobody was going to stop them.

"We play here?" asked Tom.

Lorenzo nodded his head.

"But we not have busking license."

Lorenzo reassured Tom that they didn't need any licenses to play inside a hotel. Tom was a little confused. After all he'd been arrested for playing outside on the street without a license.

"Good evening ladies and gentlemen. We are The Soul Fathers and we have been sent here by the Vatican. We are on a mission to save the world from shit music," Lorenzo announced to everybody and to nobody in particular using what he thought was a joke Pope voice.

Half way through their set a Neil Diamond tribute act arrived fully dressed for his show and stood at the bar watching. He didn't look happy. The idiot didn't realize that he was getting paid for not working.

Lorenzo was pleased that Tom was playing superbly and that they definitely would become a hit if they got the right gigs. They played for thirty minutes then took a break and went to talk to Neil Diamond.

"The agency told us you weren't coming and so we've come all the way from Santa Cruz."

"I'm not sure why Guy would have told you that."

"Guy definitely told us you were not coming," Lorenzo confirmed confidently.

Neil Diamond was confused.

"Well now that you are here you might as well play the second half," Lorenzo offered. They wouldn't be getting paid in any case and this was just an opportunity to give Tom a trial and a feel for what performing would be like.

The Soul Fathers left the hotel to the sound of Neil Diamond being crucified and walked a while under the moon until they were at the harbour where they sat down and slept behind a small wall until the sun rose to wake them.

Tom seemed unhappy, Lorenzo guessed he was clearly used to his home comforts.

"You need to use the bathroom?"

"No, me has sore head."

Lorenzo knew it was the wine. Obviously they needed to find some water to drink but they were not near any shops and they didn't have any money.

"When we get to the Karaoke Land?"

This was a good question, as Lorenzo had never ventured this far on his escapes. Also he'd never been caught so didn't know what reprisal to expect but he guessed it might be pretty severe. And so he had every intention of not getting caught.

Sunrise is around 07:30 in this part of the world at this time of year and this coincides with good and blessed people going to work. So they walked up to the main road and hitched a lift in a passing car. Clearly people were prepared to trust two priests on their mission to save the world from shit music.

They were disembarked near the banana plantation where this Good Samaritan would spend the day toiling for a small wage. After collecting his sax from the car boot Tom realised that behind the giant walls of rock and plastic there lay a forest of agriculture and he wanted to go and take a look.

They had all the time in the world and so they went inside,

where they were also offered water and strong coffee and most importantly for Tom the use of toilet facilities. Tom had plenty of suggestions on how to improve banana cultivation but fortunately no one spoke English and so they were able to leave on Lorenzo's command.

The Soul Fathers were alone in the middle of nowhere but before long a lovely couple of German tourists gave them a lift. This was perfect because they were on their way to the cable car station at El Teide. Again, dressing as papal professionals was paying dividends. The tourists spoke good English but before long Lorenzo had to stop Tom from explaining that he was from the future and that they were on the run from the penitentiary psychiatric ward.

Lorenzo diverted the conversation by telling them that Tenerife is geologically in Africa and so all the information about El Teide being the highest mountain in Spain is just confusing because Spain is in Europe not in Africa. The tourists applied their ruthless Teutonic logic and pointed out that parts of Spain are in Africa.

However El Teide is not the highest mountain in Africa either, that award goes to Kilimanjaro. El Teide is not even the highest peak in North Africa, which is less than one thousand kilometers away. That award goes to the Atlas Mountains' highest peak Toubkal. In any case El Teide is more than a mountain; it's an active volcano. Christopher Columbus described seeing a mountain of fire when he came on his journey to America in 1492. The last eruption was in 1909 although all through recorded history El Teide has been active and the main port town of Garachico was destroyed by a lava flow in 1706. This stimulated a great deal of debate in the car and passed the time.

They drove through the brutal glory of Las Cañadas, which is the cauldron of the old volcano. The sky was active with police helicopters that came buzzing low overhead. Lorenzo knew they would be conspicuous in their cassocks if they walked along the road. But they had no other clothes. Anyway, the police couldn't see them inside a car.

At the cable car station there were plenty of cars nearly all of them hire cars. Lorenzo though they wouldn't be causing too much trouble if he stole a hire car and that is exactly what he did. They only needed it for a few hours to get to Playa de Las Americas. There they could park it and forget it and eventually the hire company would recover it. Lorenzo spent five minutes looking for an unlocked hire car with the keys in the ignition. People need to take more care especially when they are on holiday unless they are hoping for an insurance claim thought Lorenzo. Tom knew nothing about insurance claims but was prepared to listen. Most people only pop out of their cars for a few minutes to take photos but obviously in this case they'd gone for a bit longer. Actually a lot longer than they had planned.

The white Seat was comfy and clean and had almost a full tank of petrol and they drove along through the splendid scenery. There were even a couple of bottles of water in the car and a packet of crisps. Life was good thought Lorenzo. Tom could not comprehend the use of cars or moving machines as he called them. Why did people want to keep moving? He couldn't understand why most of them had only one or two people in them when there was space for a few more.

Why you go in prison?" Tom asked.

Honesty is the best policy and so Lorenzo explained that he was a pyromaniac and arsonist and also an opera singer with a love of jazz and blues. But went on to explain that he was innocent of causing the fire in the hotel for which he was imprisoned. The court didn't agree and the doctors thought that it was a trauma related to a previous hotel fire where his wife was killed. They may be correct but since his wife was there with her lover, Lorenzo felt no guilt.

Lorenzo explained that he had given up opera a couple of

years ago and made a career out of Karaoke. Which as you might know is singing songs with a backing track. It's all the rage today because it allows bars to pay a small fee for a singer instead of a bigger fee for a singer and a backing band. Lorenzo could tell that a singer and a sax player would be a hit and possibly quite lucrative.

They rounded a bend near some blue-green rock formations and there was a police roadblock. As they slowed down in the queue of traffic Lorenzo frantically searched the glove compartment for the hire papers. Everybody leaves the papers in the glove compartment Lorenzo knew. Getting through the roadblock would be easy although he didn't have his driving license.

Eventually they reached the front of the queue and the police officers operating the control. Lorenzo could see a police helicopter parked by the side of the road and he knew they obviously meant business and felt confident that the police would catch them and spirit them away in the helicopter. Tom was making angry noises as he recognized the uniforms of the police who had taken him into custody. Lorenzo calmed him down and told him to stay quiet.

Lorenzo spoke in his best polite Spanish and showed them the hire car papers. They were not convinced that he was a female Norwegian tourist and so they made them park off the road near to the helicopter. Lorenzo had no need to worry about his lack of a driving license because the game was up.

They got out of the car and were being ushered towards the helicopter when Tom started remonstrating that his sax was on the back seat and that he didn't trust anybody. The helicopter pilots were chatting nearby and having a sneaky smoke, and they looked up to see two priests being escorted by the local police.

Tom hit the first police offer with the sax case and then the second knocking them both unconscious. The pilots came running towards The Soul Fathers and so The Soul Fathers ran towards them, which gave the pilots a big surprise. Tom hit them both hard on the face with the brown leather sax case again. They too were out cold on the dirt. Lorenzo could see that Tom was quite an expert with that case.

"I have learned to fly one of these in the simulator," Tom explained as he nodded towards the helicopter.

Lorenzo now had no reason to doubt him and so The Soul Fathers took to the sky. Once in the air he thought that it would have been better if they had simply taken the car, as it would be easier to abandon. It's only a few minutes flying time to Las Americas but trying to find somewhere to land before the air force intercepted and shot them down would be a little more difficult.

The view was stupendous and before long Lorenzo could see Las Americas below and could make out the circular offshore fish farms marking the surface of the sea. Even schools of whales were visible from the air with their majestic white waterspouts contrasting against the dark blue ocean.

Tom flew the chopper like a pro and they swooped down the steep side of the volcano. He circled the helicopter over the beach several times obviously looking for somewhere to land. But two priests landing a helicopter and then running away from it would attract people's attention. Then it dawned on Lorenzo that that is exactly what they needed to do. People might think it was a stunt for a movie or TV program. He didn't explain this to Tom. He just pointed to the strip of yellow sand and told him to land there.

Tom cleared the beach by flying low over it several times and then put the chopper down gently on the sand and shut down the engine.

"We go Karaoke now?" he asked with a bright smile on his face.

They walked calmly away from the chopper as the rotating blades slowed to a halt. This didn't seem dramatic enough for a film so Lorenzo left Tom standing holding the sax case and walked calmly back to the machine.

A few seconds later he came running back ran and pushed Tom on to the yellow sand. All the holidaymakers were well clear when the helicopter erupted in a massive explosion.

"Let's go and get us a beer. I need it."

They walked calmly up off the beach towards the bars with the wreckage behind them creating a pillar of dense black smoke that climbed upwards towards the sun.

6 LIVING IN LAS AMERICAS

Music: Mr Pitiful – Otis Redding

"Jesus Christ almighty I've got a mouth on me so I have, let's go in here," Lorenzo exclaimed loudly and pointed to the nearest bar.

"Beer we go for beer, what is that?"

"Holy guacamole, I explained last night. Today I show you."

The Soul Fathers walked into The Duke of Wellington and because they were in Spain Lorenzo ordered two large cervezas in English.

The barman was curious about the incident on the beach as he had heard the explosion and seen the smoke towering over the nearby buildings. He thought it was a helicopter crash. Thankfully he wasn't aware that the pilot and his passenger had been dressed in religious clothing. Lorenzo told him somebody was filming a movie.

"Are you two really priests? We don't get many of them around here. Never had one in my pub and I've been here nearly twenty-five fucking years," he told them in his broad cockney geezer accent.

Lorenzo had spent two years working in London and so he knew how to respond to his banter. Again Lorenzo decided honesty is the best policy and so he told him that they were musicians and that they were on a mission to save the world from shit music, dressed as priests. Lorenzo had Tom open the case and show him the golden sax to convince him.

"You'll have a fucking job round here then," the barman retorted loudly and with a laugh.

He introduced himself as Bob but said that everybody called him Lager Bob. He didn't explain why.

"Ok Lager Bob any idea where we can get a gig mate?"

"Yes here tomorrow night. Neil Diamond has cancelled. There's hundreds of the c@@ts on this island and most are fuckin' shit."

He was referring to the fact that there is a cornucopia of Neil Diamond tribute karaoke singers on Tenerife and that most of them are seriously lacking in ability.

"Cheers mate," Lorenzo said proudly in order to gain his confidence. In London everybody is your mate. Unless you are not. And if you are not, you are most likely a c@@t or even worse a fucking c@@t, which is a little more severe.

"You c@@ts got a factura or am I going to have to pay you black?"

But sometimes you can be a c@@t and a friend at the same time as the word can be also used as a term of endearment.

Lorenzo came clean. Not only was Lager Bob going to have to pay The Soul Fathers in cash or black to use the local terminology, but also he was going to have to give them an advance. Either that or let The Soul Fathers have some credit. Once Lager Bob had agreed to running a credit account, Lorenzo ordered them both some food. He had the T-Bone steak with chips and ordered vegetable lasagna for Tom. And of course several more beers. Things were looking good and since they owed somebody some money they were guaranteed at least one gig in order to repay the debt.

They sat at a table to eat and Lorenzo explained everything to Tom. He'd been listening intently to the conversation as it had been in English and Tom had some input to offer.

"Is good we have fucking gig tomorrow. What are we going to play you c@@t?"

This was precisely Lorenzo's concern too and so he outlined his plan. He also corrected him in the use of his recently acquired vernacular although he was impressed that Tom had learned to distinguish singular from plural. They wouldn't get far as Poor Fathers of Tenerife if one of them had a potty-mouth.

"What are you c@@ts called by the way?" Lager Bob yelled from the bar as the pub was filling up and had become rather noisy.

"The Soul Fathers mate. I'm Father Lorenzo Pitiful and this is Father Tom Perignon."

Lager Bob responded with a thumbs up and pointed to the small stage and informed that he had all the gear they needed. It was getting dark by the time they left the pub. All the police activity had subsided and the air search seemed to have been abandoned. There was also no smoke rising towards the sky from the wreckage of the police helicopter. They had nowhere to sleep and no money for a hotel so they walked towards the nightlife. It was still early though, as things don't really get jumping until after ten o'clock.

Lorenzo persuaded a lookie-lookie man to donate two black hats and some cheap sunglasses in return for taking an impromptu confession from him. These illegal street vendors are simple and honest men God bless them. Lorenzo was hoping that this slight of change of identity would help them avoid the police. Then they went in search of Irish bars where Lorenzo thought they might persuade the less simple but more optimistic Catholic customers to part with some beer and loose change.

The Soul Fathers got quite inebriated and because they had nowhere to sleep they went to lie on the beach under the diamond-studded sky to wait for the moon to cast its reflection on the inky black sea.

"What's the factura?" Tom asked sleepily.

Lorenzo explained that it's an invoice. It's a piece of paper that informs how much somebody has to pay you.

"So what's the black?"

Lorenzo explained that if you don't have a factura some establishments will pay you in cash but a little less than if you have a factura.

"Why little less?"

Patiently Lorenzo explained that if you have a factura you have to pay tax on the money you receive.

"What is the money and what is the tax?"

Exasperated, Lorenzo went on to further explain that money is something that you get given for doing something. You then use the money to buy goods and services. And that tax is money that the government takes from people to pay for goods and services that they provide.

"What is the government?"

Lorenzo had to think this one through before he answered. His thoughts were that in so-called Western Democracies we have government of the people for the people by the people. He believed that is the standard explanation and that is the one he offered him.

"The people get some of the people to take the tax from the people and use it to provide the goods and the services for the people?"

"Yes more or less," Lorenzo answered.

Tom gave up at this point and went to sleep. He was lucky at least he had his sax case to use as a pillow thought Lorenzo. Lorenzo couldn't sleep and was surprised to see the beach slowly fill with people. He noticed that mostly they were families with children.

Lorenzo decided that they needed a bonfire and so he went to collect some old pallet wood and cardboard boxes. Once he had the fire going he felt very satisfied, he liked the glow of a warm fire at night-time, and several people came to sit nearby and Lorenzo chatted at length. They were concerned about the environment and disgusted that a film crew had left a burning helicopter further along the beach. Most of the day when not working these people passed their time clearing the beach of plastic debris that had washed up on the shore.

He discovered that all the people there at night are homeless because they cannot earn enough money to rent accommodation nearby. The cost and time involved in commuting from where homes are cheaper prohibits doing that. These are the low-paid minimum-wage hotel workers that keep the island tourist economy ticking over.

Lorenzo woke Tom and as he had decided to entertain the audience. He wasn't worried about the two-hour set they were to play tomorrow and he had all of the songs that he wanted to play on his phone and he was sure that Tom could play them. But this was a great opportunity to have a rehearsal.

He borrowed a small portable speaker to amplify the backing tracks on his phone and they played the planned set. The small crowd loved the signature tune Mr Pitiful originally by Otis Redding. Overall the set went well and it was a good rehearsal and everybody wanted to dance. Tom could really play that golden sax too; he was amazing considering he is only about three years old. Lorenzo remembered that his dog was older than that and wondered how Pancho was doing with his new owner. It made him a little sad.

Tom also noticed that there were a massive number of people sleeping on the beach and asked why it was so busy at night. He couldn't understand why they had nowhere to live. And when Lorenzo explained that they didn't have enough money to rent somewhere to live he couldn't understand why they were working in a place where they couldn't afford to survive. He seemed very concerned that the small people as he called the children had no home.

"Do these people get paid in the black or do they use the factura?" Tom asked angrily.

"No they have the tax taken from them every time they get paid, which is normally at the end of the month. They are not paid black and are not paid with factura,"

Lorenzo was finding his line of questioning very challenging.

"Don't you have money or tax in the future?"

"No need money, no need tax, no need government. We have one central controller, which is an intelligent machine. You people very primitive and barbaric," he scolded.

Tom thought out loud "these people not paid every day? They need to wait until end of month for money that is not enough to live on and then the government of the people for the people takes some of it and doesn't help them have home for them and their little people?"

Lorenzo could see Tom's mind working overtime trying to understand the absurdity of the situation.

"The government of the people by the people just takes the money without asking?" Tom emphasized.

"Yes."

"But this is the theft. I learned about the theft in the penitentiary. That taking the thing or the money without the permission is the theft. The government of the people by the people is making the theft. Yes or not?"

Lorenzo just nodded. Tom's logic was impeccable.

"What do you use to pay for stuff you want to buy?" Lorenzo enquired regarding transactions in the future.

Tom really didn't understand the concept of money and taxation but the more Lorenzo thought about it the more he realized he'd just kind of accepted things himself and didn't really understand it either. But Tom had a great idea. He thought that they should make money from playing music and then buy all the homeless workers somewhere to live. That The Soul Fathers should become the providers of this service. That The Soul Fathers should become the government of the people for these people.

It wasn't as stupid as it sounded but the idea has sort of been tried before. Some people call it a church. And so a plan was hatched to create The Church of the Soul Fathers. That name would do for now until they could come up with another more appropriate name and Lorenzo went to sleep on the idea.

7 EVERYDAY PEOPLE

Music: Everyday People – Sly & the family Stone

The Soul Fathers had a chilled day wandering around Las Americas collecting money dressed as priests for the everyday people of The Church of The Soul Fathers and for some beer for themselves too. The idea for The Church of The Soul Fathers was taking shape and Lorenzo thought they might be able to finance the purchase of a couple of apartment blocks that he'd seen for sale. Perhaps it could be called The Hard Knock Hotel or maybe The Soul Village.

Later they found a nice little place for a spot of pesto and pasta and Lorenzo introduced Tom to the delights of more ice cream. Tom wondered if it was possible to combine the two and create pesto ice cream. This Lorenzo thought was a brilliant idea. Tom was clearly a marketing genius. After a rest on the beach where they watched the peaches sunbathing, The Soul Fathers headed for the Duke of Wellington and their next gig.

The pub was very busy and it seemed that Lager Bob had pulled out all the stops and people were looking forward to seeing The Soul Fathers live.

"Right you c@@ts I hope you are ready? When are you starting?" Lager Bob's voice cut through the commotion.

There was a gang of fifteen Gary Glitters in the audience. As it turned out they were fifteen lads from Sunderland on a stag weekend. Tom was eyeing them quizzically. He thought that they were clones like him. Lorenzo couldn't imagine a world populated with groups of people all looking the same but there he was, surrounded by identical Gary Glitters.

"Lager Bob, I thought we were on at nine thirty?" Lorenzo shouted to the bar.

"Just get the show started you fucking clock watcher," was his cordial response.

"Why aye lad are ye actually a Catholic priest?" asked one of the Gary Glitters.

"No we are not. It's just a show. We are musicians."

"At least ye are not kiddie fiddlers then," and the leader of the gang let out a crazy laugh to which the rest joined in.

"Do ye take requests?" another called.

Lorenzo couldn't wait for the punch line. But it came anyway.

"Don't play messin' with the kid."

They all laughed so much at this Lorenzo thought they were going to die collectively of heart attacks like in some sort of religious ritual suicide.

You don't get many hecklers at the opera but Lorenzo had learned the art of how to deal with them on the karaoke circuit.

"Ma vaffanculo." It wasn't a very witty response but Lorenzo really wasn't in the mood.

The Soul Fathers got on the small stage made from some pallet wood and did their first half of the show. Part way through there was a commotion outside that Lager Bob had to go and sort out. It was obviously a problem because that's the only reason you carry a baseball bat to the main entrance of the establishment you manage. Lager Bob didn't seem to mind a spot of action even though he's about seventy years old.

They went to the bar for more beer at the interval and Lager Bob was so impressed with their performance that he offered to be their manager. He said he could get them lots of gigs and make them pots of dosh. It seemed like an offer they couldn't refuse.

Gary Glitter or at least one of them who Lorenzo guessed was the leader of the gang gave his testimony on the quality of last night's act. He wasn't impressed with Neil Diamond either.

"Watch your mouth. If you don't like it piss off. I've had your money anyway you c@@t," Lager Bob retorted.

Fiscal planning was obviously a strong point for Lager Bob and Lorenzo was warming to his abrasive attitude and so he tried to diffuse the situation by asking one of the Glitter gang what they did for a living in Sunderland.

"Why aye man we used to be coal miners like, but now we are cryptocurrency miners. We work out of a Portakabin in the city center man."

Lorenzo wondered if they could help create a cryptocurrency to build The Hard Knock Hotel. They seemed interested to assist after it had been explained about the plight of the homeless minimum-wage workers on the beach. They agreed to meet next day in the American Diner across the street at lunchtime.

Lager Bob had enlisted the assistance of the Hell's Angels earlier to prevent a gang of Neil Diamond tribute acts from entering The Duke of Wellington. They helped fill the bar after the departure of the Gary Glitters who were headed down to the Bull's Head in The Patch to watch the Vagabonds, the best band in Tenerife the Glitters had said. Lorenzo guessed that he and Tom Perignon could oust them from that position. Lager Bob said the Hell's Angels helped him out a lot with his charity events. Lorenzo thought that they seemed kind hearted and they loved The Soul Father's music.

Close to the end of the second set Tom left the stage abruptly. Lorenzo thought that he had bowel problems again due to his change of diet. At the same time a group dressed as Elvis had come in the bar, about ten men all dressed identical except for one whose clothes were the reverse of the others. His were black with white piping whereas the others wore white with black piping. Lorenzo had assumed they were there to watch the Neil Diamond tribute that had been cancelled. And to be fair Lorenzo thought that they looked quite similar in their rhinestone-studded stage gear.

Tom came out of the toilets after they had gone. Lorenzo was talking to Lager Bob about the Hard Knock Hotel and The Church of The Soul Fathers. He seemed really keen to help them help everyday people.

"If you are gonna take a shit you do it in your own time you prick. Don't you ever fuckin' get off the stage before the end, you fucking hear?" he bawled at Tom. He was concerned about Tom's casual attitude but Tom didn't seem to hear or care.

Lager Bob had made his position clear. But Lorenzo could tell that he really was a big softie with a heart of gold. Except following their gig they still owed him money after deductions for yesterday's bar bill and hire of the equipment for tonight's gig. Lager Bob had said he had the gear but hadn't told them he was charging them for using it.

They agreed to meet tomorrow in the American Diner to sign contracts.

And so the duo left The Duke of Wellington and strolled to their accommodation on the beach with the other homeless workers.

8 AT THE HARD LUCK CAFÉ

Music : Money (That's what I want) – Junior Walker

The pair strolled along the Paseo Las Vistas looking at the yellow sand and the wrecked helicopter still sitting there. It was a beautiful morning and the sun was beating down on their priestly black attire. Lorenzo could see the Torres De Sol in the distance and knew in his heart of hearts that their mission was to buy or build something similar for the homeless workers.

The Hard Luck Café was nearby and so they went the long way round and got there at the appointed time.

Tom's face lit up in wonder at all the retro Americana in the café and in particular the vintage juke box standing in the corner complete with 45's. They had lots of change because they'd been collecting for The Church of The Soul Fathers as they walked. But they didn't need it because Lorenzo showed Tom how to operate the jukebox for free with a single slap on the front of the machine. He then grabbed a huge red faux leather corner seat with enough space for them all and sat to wait for the Glitter Gang.

It didn't take long but Lorenzo was surprised to see them pile inside still dressed in their costumes from the night before.

"Sorry bonnie lad, we seem to have lost one last night but never mind he's just the electrician. This cryptocurrency shite uses up a lot of juice and so we always blame him." Then added "The twat," for emphasis.

Lorenzo outlined his proposal that he needed to raise a couple of million Euros in order buy and renovate or build from scratch. He favoured the former because the process of getting planning permission was known to be lengthy and costly in Tenerife.

Tom joined the table and wanted to eat ice cream and so Lorenzo ordered everyone some milk shakes. Tom's face light up with delight at the taste of the chocolate drink.

The Glitter gang ordered the biggest cheeseburgers on the menu and Tom looked visibly sick when he discovered it was cow and cheese and pig in a bun.

Ian was the spokesman for the Glitter gang and corrected Lorenzo when he called him Gary. He explained the process of issuing a cryptocurrency.

"First of all we start with an Initial Coin Offering or ICO. Lets call this currency Dream Token for example. So early investors will buy Dream Tokens at a huge discount on the face value. Lets say the face value is one Euro and the ICO lets them have them for 50 Euro cents. This means we can raise some real cash. But the ultimate problem is that." Ian was interrupted.

Lager Bob pushed everybody along the seat a bit and nodded to Ian saying "carry on son, I'm listening."

"The big problem is that is that it leaves people and organisations holding Dream Tokens and these will fluctuate in value and so we may not be able to fulfil our obligations."

Lager Bob took over.

"An ICO is like crowd-funding and it leaves the participants on one side with some sort of reward with the issuer holding cash. For example sponsoring a new film might get the participants a voucher that allows free access to the Premiere. So what do the participants get as a reward?"

"I hadn't imagined they would get anything. I was just hoping that they wanted to be charitable," Lorenzo answered.

Tom had to be excused from the table. Lorenzo watched him head for the bathrooms and knew that Tom had overdone it with the milkshakes. Four is really too much. But reflected that he's only behaving like any three-year old would.

Bob was just about to resume control of the conversation when the Neil Diamonds burst into the café.

"What do you c@@ts want now," roared Lager Bob as he stood up to face them off.

The leader of the Neil Diamonds whose name Lorenzo later discovered was Alan didn't get the chance to answer because the Gary Glitters leapt across the table and got stuck in and a brawl broke out.

"Stop," roared Lager Bob at the top of his voice so he could be heard over the din of the jukebox.

Remarkably the fighting stopped as quickly as it had started.

"Sit down boys," he ordered to the Gary Glitter Gang.

Lager Bob pointed outside through the huge windows obscured with sign lettering to the forty or so Hell's Angels revving up their motorbikes.

"If you want any trouble go outside and talk to those guys. They'll be very happy to assist you. Now fuck off."

Lager Bob turned his back on the Neil Diamonds and they shuffled out meekly as he sat down again.

The leader of the Neil Diamonds pleaded with Lager Bob. "We have families to support. We need the work."

"Listen," said Lager Bob as he ignored their pleas.

"Yes mate," answered Lorenzo.

"It's quite simple. Were you going to charge the tenants rent to live at the Hard Knock Hotel or not?"

"No I hadn't planned on it."

"Well you need to. It's basic human nature. People don't respect anything that's free."

Lorenzo agreed with him.

"With the rent coming in then you have an income and therefore you have a business and so you should be able to borrow money for the accommodation. Take out a mortgage or something."

"True," Lorenzo acknowledged. And then added "But we will need a deposit in order to get a loan. Maybe we can do that with a cryptocurrency?"

"Listen bonnie lad. Just forget about Dream Token. Cryptos are a big con, just like real money." Ian finished his statement with a laugh. "It will be easier and quicker to rob a casino," he suggested.

Lorenzo thought that on the face of it this actually was a good idea, "Where's the nearest casino?"

Not far," replied Lager Bob and added "just around the corner, run by Ruskies. The fucking c@@ts. Need taking down a peg or two."

The table went quiet and they all looked at each other.

"You c@@ts know how to beat the house?" Lager Bob enquired enthusiastically.

"Yes bonnie lad, this one here has been to university and is a mathematics genius. He's the one that wrote all our algorithms for our cryptomining like," said Ian as he nodded to the Gary Glitter whose real name was actually Gary.

"Okay meet me at my place tonight at ten and we'll go a-gambling gentlemen," suggested Lager Bob.

Lager Bob handed Lorenzo their contracts saying, "here sign these. Only one of you c@@ts needs to sign."

"What's happened to the other c@@t?" He added after he had looked around for a few seconds.

Lorenzo had overlooked the fact that Tom had been missing for some time and got up to check the bathroom as the Gary Glitters left telling him they would see them later.

Tom came out of the toilets and walked towards the table. Lorenzo could see he looked terrible. He was significantly fatter and he now had a white beard and long shoulder length grey hair and looked twenty years older.

Lager Bob walked past informing that he'd see them at The Duke of Wellington later and that he had to meet his daughter. He hadn't noticed the change in Tom's appearance.

As he got to the door he told Lorenzo that the church idea was a good one. Especially if it was set up all legal and proper as a charity.

"What do you plan to call it?"

"The Church of The Soul Fathers."

Lager Bob didn't think that was a good name.

"The Church for Everyday People sounds better. Leave it with me I'll get my lawyer to sort it out," he said as he closed the door behind him.

"I've had another attack," Tom said as he sat down slowly.

"I can see that. But what's causing it?"

"I don't know but I'm ageing very quickly. You know I am engineered with the dropDead@40.gene?"

"Yes you mentioned it."

"Well I don't want to drop dead just yet and certainly not here."

"What do you think is causing it?" Lorenzo repeated.

"No idea. It could be anything. The diet, something in the air. This is uncharted territory for me."

Tom was right this was indeed uncharted territory. Somebody from the future comes to the past. A clone from the future comes to the past. Something from the future comes to the past. Lorenzo was equally as confused.

"We better get you a haircut and a shave."

Tom agreed and so they went to find the Turkish barber. Lorenzo liked the Turkish barbers because they burn the hair off your ears using fire.

As they walked Tom explained that he needed to get back to the future before he died of old age but that he wanted to stay and help the homeless people especially the children. Lorenzo wasn't sure how long it would take to do that and was concerned that they now had signed contracts with Lager Bob.

9 JOY CASINO DEL SUR

Music: Joy Part 1 – Isaac Hayes

There was a show starting in the casino when they arrived there. The Gary Glitter Gang who were still in costume, crowded round the cage like a pack of wolves and were whistling and cat calling. The manager came over to calm them down. He pointed to the row of bouncers at the back but this did nothing to cool their ardour because the bouncers were the Neil Diamonds from earlier in the day who were now reduced to working as security for the Russian Mafia.

The spotlights lit up the mirrored glass ball hanging from the ceiling, which in turn scattered the light across the dancer in the cage. She was a beautiful woman with her blond hair cut in a blunt bob. She didn't recognize Lorenzo but he instantly knew her and his heart skipped a beat. It skipped another one when she turned to face him. This time instead of a nun's habit she was wearing a gold leotard that exposed most of her breasts. And on those magnificent breasts she had something Lorenzo had never imagined. She had a tattoo of that ancient symbol of protection, royal power, and good health, The Eye of Horus.

Lager Bob had brought his daughter Rita with him and he

sent her to round up the Gary Glitters. One of them was needed to help beat the house. Lager Bob went to have a look at the dancer and as he got closer to the cage he turned round and winked at Lorenzo and nodded indicating his sexual appreciation for the acrobat and dancer Martina Topolova of the Topolova Twins.

Lorenzo succumbed to his animal impulses and walked up to the cage. He took off his hat and sunglasses and wiped the sweat from his forehead. She smiled and winked at him before she immediately commenced her acrobatic show with her twin brother.

Tom had taken a place at the roulette table and when Lorenzo reluctantly returned, they swapped places and Tom stood behind him with Lager Bob and Rita.

The plan was a simple one. Tony, one of the Gary Glitters would place an inside bet, a bet on an exact number and Lorenzo was to place a bet on the next number. Tony was receiving signals on the phone in his pocket from Gary the Makem Mathematician. All Tony needed to do was count the vibrations of the phone. So if he placed a bet on red one Lorenzo would place a bet on black two. This worked because Tony placed a small bet, which he lost and Lorenzo placed a significantly larger one on the winning number. In order to not look too successful Tony gave some bad bets but overall Lorenzo was way ahead after thirty minutes. And after one hour Lorenzo was up by over half a million Euros because the house did not operate betting limits. Enough for the Hard Knock Hotel project to get started.

"We need to ask you to leave the table padre," the husky Russian voice whispered into Lorenzo's ear. When he looked round he saw standing next to him the proprietress of the Joy Casino.

"Aha the Russian Mafia at last." Lorenzo smiled and looked into the woman's brown eyes and slightly Asiatic face. She clearly had some Siberian blood in her. She was very beautiful and a woman with authority and dignity aged about sixty-five years old.

She introduced herself as The Babushka and told him that she had no links with those kreemeenahlz as she pronounced it.

Lorenzo gallantly left the table as requested and handed Tom some chips and he slipped into the vacant seat.

Lorenzo went over to catch the end of Martina's show but he was too late and next up was a Neil Diamond tribute karaoke singer who was terrible. So Lorenzo wandered over to the bar and ordered a cocktail. Then Rita slid into the seat next to him and ordered another cocktail. She was a pretty petite brunette with a French accent. Lorenzo learned that she was the brains behind Lager Bob's business empire and had been marketing manager for a soap manufacturer in her native Brussels. She was Lager Bob's secret love child. Lorenzo was saddened to learn that her mother had died in a hotel fire in Italy a few years back.

Rita explained that her lawyers had created a limited company charity for The Church for Everyday People. She said she'd send an invoice because people never appreciate things that are free. She said it wasn't too much, only twenty thousand euros and they had twenty-eight days to pay. So now The Soul Fathers had to earn over seven hundred euros per day just to stand still. Running a church was an expensive business it would appear. Rita was just like her father but a lot sexier. Lorenzo considered that they hadn't even started but the bills were mounting up already and he felt sick. He also needed a piss, so on the way to the toilet he checked up on Tom. He was being just as successful as he had been and The Babushka had taken quite a shine to him and was sitting next to him chatting in Russian. That boy's list of talents was quite impressive thought Lorenzo.

All of the other players at the table were dressed as Elvis Presley and were in identical costumes except for one and Lorenzo realized these were the same ones that turned up at last night's gig. There was no Tony Glitter at the table as The Babushka had removed him earlier and Tom was winning by his own skill and judgment.

Lorenzo noticed that the Elvis gang seemed to be following Tom's bets some of the time. And when they did, they lost. The Elvis in black shouted over to him that he wanted the sax returned and Lorenzo felt that Tom had some explaining to do.

When Lorenzo returned from the bathroom Tom was at the bar with The Babushka and Martina Topolova. Lorenzo received a lovey warm cuddle from Martina but she couldn't hang around, as she had to get back to Santa Cruz to go to work in the morning. But she did briefly explain that she was working for free at the hospital and wasn't actually a nun, and that she only wore the uniform. Her real job was as an acrobat in the show with her brother.

The Babushka departed and Lorenzo and Tom were left alone.

"OK who are the Elvis gang and why are they asking for your sax?"

"That's Prof. #ELv15 in the black from the music academy. He's from the future. I stole the sax from the music museum there. The others are his assistants. He comes here to sing karaoke in bars."

Lorenzo was impressed by his frankness.

"Anything else?"

"Yes, I smashed the deputy's head in with Jimi Hendrix's guitar. But I did not kill him. I swear I didn't."

This sounded like a familiar story to Lorenzo and possibly one that Bob Marley might have been proud of if it had also involved the sheriff and a gun.

"So they want the sax returned and they came here to track me down. They want me to go back to the future to be executed for killing the deputy."

Lorenzo was surprised that there wasn't going to be a trial.

"If I stay here I'm going to die of old age and if I go back to the future I'm going to get executed."

Lorenzo thought about this for a moment. He's got dropDead@40.gene and so he knows when he is going to die but is worried about getting executed. Strange logic he thought.

"Don't worry about the sax. You can get another one here. It's no big deal," Lorenzo offered. As an afterthought he added, "Nobody dies of old age you know. Old age is not a disease. You can't catch it off toilet seats."

"Sax very special. Belong to a president of United States of America."

At that moment the fire alarm sounded and Lorenzo could smell the familiar odour of smoke.

The casino was evacuated and they all stood around in groups out in the night air whilst they waited for the fire brigade to tackle the blaze.

The fire got significantly worse and the police came and Lorenzo and Tom moved discreetly away just in case they were recognised.

They went to find The Babushka so that they could cash in their chips but she politely fobbed them off. It then dawned on Lorenzo that all they had was worthless plastic chips and with the casino burned to the ground there was not much chance of them seeing their winnings in real money.

10 THE IN CROWD

Music: In With The In Crowd – Dobie Gray

"You alright son? You look different." Lager Bob nodded in the direction of Tom. Only now had he noticed the physical change that had taken place.

However Lager Bob himself didn't look any different. He was still wearing a ghastly checked jacket and sunglasses with his strawberry blond hair slicked back close to his head. Lorenzo thought that he must have been roasting in that jacket. It looked really warm. Too warm for Tenerife.

Lorenzo and Tom sat in The Duke with Lager Bob and ran through their options. Lager Bob offered to send the Hell's Angels round to collect their winnings but Lorenzo politely declined his offer because he felt guilty about the fire. He hadn't expected the whole place to burn down.

Rita arrived and listened silently to their discussions. She concluded that The Babushka would have the money in the safe and so they should go and collect it. But then added that if she wasn't insured then she'd need the cash to build a new casino and she doubted if the Russians ever bought insurance of the conventional kind.

Lorenzo thought about it for a few minutes and agreed to let the Hell's Angels collect the cash on commission.

"Tom where are the chips?" Lorenzo asked.

"What chips? Small plastic coins from casino?" Tom looked innocently into Lorenzo's brown eyes.

"Yes those are the ones," Lager Bob answered lowly.

"Put in trash."

"Where?" Lorenzo asked firmly.

"After big fire when we outside casino. No have pockets so just put in trash."

"You stupid c@@t," Rita concluded firmly. She had taken the words right out of her father's mouth and Lorenzo's too.

"Lorenzo say it only a game," he pleaded.

That was that. No chips no money. No money no honey. Back to the drawing board again thought Lorenzo.

Lager Bob said it was pointless going back to the casino to look for them as the bins were emptied every morning and it was now after one pm.

"We could always organize a benefit concert," offered Rita.

"We'll need to put a band together. With a horn section and backing singers," Lorenzo contributed.

Tom's face lit up with excitement and he stood up and punched the air with both hands and shouted "YEAH. Get up like a sex machine."

"And guitar and bass and drums," Lorenzo continued with equal enthusiasm.

"And funky organ player," offered Tom excitedly.

"Yeah keyboards," Lorenzo confirmed.

"Two tenors an alto and a baritone, trumpet, trombone and female singers," Tom demanded.

That was an impressive line-up. Tenerife is full of musicians and some are quite good. But could they get this line up?

"Let's start with a guitarist. Do you know any that are available?" Lorenzo asked.

"Yes I know a really good guitarist. A Cuban. In retirement but might be persuaded," suggested Rita.

"And where can we see this guitarist?"

"At the Buddhist monastery near here," she advised.

"Is he any good?"

"She's fucking excellent."

"SHE?" A Cuban Buddhist nun on guitar," Lorenzo considered this risible.

Lager Bob informed them that he would hire them a car so that they had some transport. Lorenzo guessed it would all go on the bill at the end of the day. But some wheels would be nice he thought.

"Can we get a Hummer, please?"

Lager Bob stared back across the table at Lorenzo. Lorenzo knew by his look that was a no.

"Listen you c@@t, you'll get what you're given."

Lorenzo really thought a Hummer suited the image. The Soul Wagon had to be a giant Tonka toy.

"Listen son you're supposed to be running a fucking church."

Lorenzo knew that Lager Bob had a point.

"A Humvee, only Neil Diamond tributes have Hummers," Lager Bob reminded him in an exasperated tone of voice.

"Victoria knows a good bass player and drummer. Go and meet her. The three of them are all at the monastery," advised Rita.

"When we do this concert?" asked Tom. And then added "I need to go back to." But Lorenzo interrupted him.

"He needs to get back home. A family emergency."

"Listen son you're under contract. Don't start to fuck me around."

Honesty is always the best policy and so I explained about Tom's problems in a way that I thought Lager Bob might understand.

"OK that's it. You're off the payroll," said Lager Bob.

"What?" Lorenzo shouted back.

"Contracts null and void. Fuck off the pair of you."

"No contract very good opportunity. Now you pay us the black not the factura?" Tom's logic was impeccable as usual.

"Shut this twat up will you son,"

"Singers are ten a penny and I can get another sax player. But you've given me a good idea. I think this is a money spinner," Lager Bob announced.

"We are The Soul Fathers. Nobody else can be us you old," and Lorenzo searched his vocabulary for the word. And the word was

"C@@T."

"Soul Fathers, Soul Fuckers. Fuck off." It was Lager Bob's turn to get angry now.

"Listen daddy, please don't be so hasty."

Lager Bob relaxed a bit and his face lost some its redness. His daughter's pleading seemed to have worked.

"We've all got problems. It wasn't so long ago that I was one of yours," she reminded him.

Lager Bob put his arm around her shoulder and hugged his little girl and gave her a peck on the cheek.

"Come back tomorrow morning gentlemen and I'll sort the car out. I'll introduce you to the keyboard player too. He works at the car hire."

"Are you talking about Ebony Tony?" Lorenzo knew Tony and was looking after his dog Pancho. They had worked together before. Tony had left his wife and was now working at a car hire as well as doing gigs in the evening with his new woman.

11 THE SOUL WAGON

Music: (I'm a) Road Runner – Junior Walker

Lager Bob's business partner Guy was too busy in the kitchen to act as chauffeur and so Rita drove them to the car hire in an old black Mercedes S500. This was one of Lager Bob's status symbols. The gold sovereign rings and chain were his other visible signs of success. The air conditioning didn't work but otherwise it was very comfy.

Another less obvious status symbol was Lager Bob's choice of business partner. Guy was from Tenerife and had been educated in the U.S.A. He had a whole host of business degrees from prestigious universities. He was the real brains behind Lager Bob's business operation it would seem, and Rita looked up to him.

The Fiat 500 is possibly the most European car Lorenzo could think of. An Italian classic now made in Poland because labour costs are cheaper there. The factory that took the jobs from Italy was funded by an EU grant financed obviously by those same Italian taxpayers that lost their jobs. Conceived originally as a city car it had a 500cc engine for years, but today the engine is more than twice that size thus demonstrating that consumption increases, as we get wealthier.

The car hire shop wasn't one of your mainstream franchises, it was one of Lager Bob's enterprises and it was a rent-a-wreck business. And so what they were given was a Fiat 500 the same age as Lorenzo, in sun-faded black with white doors. The doors were not original and the rest was shabby like an ancient nun's habit. There was no air-con and inside it stank of piss.

But it was nice for Lorenzo to meet Ebony Tony and see Pancho. And moreover Pancho was happy to see Lorenzo.

Pancho is part Irish wolfhound and part English sheepdog. A sort of Anglo-Irish Wolfdog in Sheepdog's clothing. And he's pretty big. Too big for the back seat of a Fiat 500. But Lorenzo couldn't just leave him with Tony. And Tony didn't want Lorenzo to leave without him and neither did Pancho.

Tom had never seen a dog before and would have been happy for Pancho to have been left behind with Tony.

"We take this Pancho dog for eating him?"

"No, Pancho is a pet. We feed him."

"We feed him dead animal too?"

Lorenzo just nodded. What else could he do?

So they drove away from the shabby back street car lot in some dingy pueblo in the South of the island. Lorenzo wasn't sure that The Soul Wagon was going to get them very far, but since they were still homeless The Soul Fathers were not constrained by needing to get anywhere special. Lager Bob remained behind to count the week's takings.

Lorenzo had explained the charitable venture to Tony. He said that he had some musician friends working for a holiday company and they would make up a complete horn section. They all worked at Tenerife South airport, which was nearby. But he also advised that they should talk to the Tenerife Family Church because they were well established on the island and had been doing good work for years. He recommended going to Costa del Silencio and asking for Pastor Bill.

The Soul Wagon smoked its way along the TF-1, which is the motorway to the airport.

"Keep your eyes on that black Hummer behind us," Lorenzo told Tom.

"Lager Bob said Hummers are only for likes of Neil Diamonds so maybe they be following us?"

Pancho sat in the back stinking silently.

"There are more, three I think," observed Tom.

The Neil Diamonds had come out in force, if indeed it was the rhinestone security guards. However at the junction for the airport where they turned off the motorway, the convoy drove straight ahead.

The Soul Wagon headed for the airport terminal and disgorged The Soul Fathers in the drop off zone where no waiting was allowed. The three of them marched into the Departures hall. Two fake priests and a real big dog. They were looking for a holiday company opposite gate thirty. Ebony Tony couldn't remember the name of the organisation the musicians worked for and hoped that at least one of them would be on shift when Lorenzo went there. He had given Lorenzo their names on a bit of paper so he went to gate thirty and asked at the service window opposite for three saxophone players, a trombonist and a trumpeter.

Tom was the alto player and he came out to explain that the others were on different shift patterns.

Lorenzo introduced Tom the alto player to Tom the tenor player.

"Tom not my name. Not really. We not have names we have hashtags, mine #TMp319."

"What is he talking about?" Tom the alto player asked bluntly.

"He's not been himself recently. Just ignore Father Tom," Lorenzo said with the emphasis on 'Father Tom'.

Alto Tom agreed to put the Jet Free Horns together and meet them at The Duke of Wellington. But he wasn't too sure about getting everybody in the horn section together at the same time, which would of course be a problem for rehearsals and any gigs. He was the exception he told them, as he had been sacked for informing his manager of the company's failure to obey EU Employment Law. He had refused to work sixty hours per week because it was illegal and also because he was only paid for forty. Today would be his last day in the job as he had been dismissed for making this observation.

"He also need wait month end for pay and then government steal from him the money tax?"

Lorenzo nodded in agreement.

"And also his boss steals time from him by making him work more hours than he paid to do?"

"Yes," and Lorenzo nodded again in agreement.

"Not very good civilization have you created in this place have you?"

Lorenzo thought it was a fair comment.

Lorenzo decided to go next to Costa del Silencio to meet Pastor Bill but when The Soul Wagon hit the TF-1 they were immediately shadowed by those same three black Hummers.

12 BUILDING A COMMUNITY

Music: A Change Is Gonna Come – Sam Cooke

The Tenerife Family Church was found very easily. It was downstairs in the Centro Commercial in Costa del Silencio, which is a small town near the airport. It doesn't look much like a church. It looks more like a shop, because it was commercial unit.

Pastor Bill was in his office in the rear and Lorenzo and Tom went and knocked on his door. They were invited in and they introduced themselves. Pastor Bill got up from behind his desk and patted Pancho and offered them a seat.

"I've seen you guys before."

"Where?" Lorenzo asked.

"You were at the Russian Casino when it burned down the other night. Saw your photo in the paper."

Lorenzo and Tom sat erect in the seats and still had their cassocks, hats and glasses on. They were The Soul Fathers after all. Lorenzo became concerned that the police would resume their search for them.

"Fire brigade says it was arson."

"Really" Lorenzo restrained a laugh.

"Pity about the fatality."

"Fatality? Who? I thought everybody had got out."

"There were some acrobats doing a show one of them is reported missing by her brother."

Lorenzo sat still and said, "Did they find the remains?"

"Not sure. It was a pretty serious blaze. Everything was destroyed."

This all came as a shock to Lorenzo and Tom.

"I saw their show a few weeks ago there. What did you think?" asked Pastor Bill.

"We only saw the start, we were more interested in the roulette wheel."

Pastor Bill described the Topolova twin's show, which involved one scene where Martina acted as a rag doll and was wheeled on stage in a suitcase by her brother. He opened the suitcase and out flopped Martina who was then contorted into various positions.

Lorenzo realized that he wanted to be the one to help contort her into various positions. But now that was never going to happen.

"Anyway, how can we help you Fathers?"

Lorenzo was still in shock but he outlined the plan to build The Hard Knock Hotel using the proceeds from a benefits concert. He left out the bit about setting up a church. Although he included the bit about involving a cryptocurrency.

Pastor Bill thought it was a great idea but doubted that one single benefits concert would generate enough money for a project of this size.

"I like the Dream Token idea. So let's consider the Dream Token Presale & ICO simply as a means to raise cash to get this off the ground, say 35% of issuance. This will lead to price discovery of Dream Token on secondary markets."

Pastor Bill was pretty switched on.

"I like the name too. We can make wishes come true. Dream Token needs to be both a utility token and a store of value. Do you understand about money and community?"

"Eh not really," Lorenzo said honestly.

"Money as an agreement is always valid only within a given community. The Benedictine order specifies that communitas is created by the way the economic necessities of the monastery are organised. The monks should be self-sufficient as a group but totally interdependent amongst themselves."

The Soul Fathers sat quietly and nodded in unison.

"There's a general rule that says whenever money gets involved, communities break down. The Benedictine rule prohibits monetary exchanges between members of the community although between the community and the outside world it is accepted as a necessity in order to acquire additional resources. To understand how community is lost we must understand how it is created. Anthropologists have discovered that community does not necessarily arise out of proximity, otherwise a 200-story tower block in a big city would produce community. Similarly, common language, religion, culture, and even blood, doesn't automatically create community although all of these factors can clearly play a support role in the process, the key ingredient is something else."

"Which is?" Lorenzo asked enthusiastically.

"Community is based on reciprocity of gift exchanges. It is a process not a thing."

They waited silently for him to proceed.

"Imagine that you need a box of nails and you pop to the hardware shop to buy one. There is no expectation either by you or the shopkeeper that any future reciprocity is involved. This is one of the main reasons why monetary exchanges are so efficient. But whilst each transaction stands on its own, no community has been created either."

"OK," Lorenzo offered so that Pastor Bill knew he had an attentive audience.

"Now imagine that you go out for another box of nails and that your neighbour is sitting on his porch. When you tell him that you are off to buy a box of nails he tells you that he has a spare box he can give you and refuses to take the money you offer him. The gift of the box of nails is a community building transaction, because firstly you're sure to say 'hello' next time you see each other and secondly when the neighbour rings your door late on a Saturday night asking if you have any sugar you are sure to reciprocate."

"I see," said Lorenzo because he did see.

"The purchase of a box of nails from a shop would not create the same effect because a commercial transaction is a closed system i.e. the nails for the money. A gift in contrast is an open system because it leaves an imbalance that some future transaction completes. The gift of a box of nails is a community building transaction since a new thread is woven into the societal fabric. But you don't need an anthropologist to tell you about the relationship between gifts and community building. The etymology of the word 'community' provides the answer."

Tom interrupted, "The word 'Community' derives from two Latin roots: cum meaning together or among each other; and munere meaning to give. 'Community' therefore means to give among each other."

"Exactly Father," confirmed Pastor Bill, "A community is therefore a group that relates to itself."

Lorenzo and Tom both nodded in agreement and Lorenzo was impressed by both Tom's and Pastor Bill's knowledge.

"Philanthropists will be able to sponsor a dream by making a pledge in Fiat currency. By Fiat I mean real wonga. We can call them Dream Makers. The first dream we will make come true can be The Hard Knock Hotel."

To Lorenzo his sounded very interesting and quite exciting.

"The money from your benefit concert can be used to kick start the presale. What do you think?"

"Holy guacamole this is brilliant," Lorenzo replied enthusiastically.

"I hope also that this can change the poor image of cryptocurrencies," Pastor Bill concluded.

"We should consider community not as a state but as a process. If it is not nourished by regular reciprocal exchanges it will decay and die. A community can therefore be defined as a group of people who honour each other's gifts, and who trust that all each others' gifts will be reciprocated in some way one day. This will be the job of the church," he finalised.

"Amen brother, I mean Pastor," Lorenzo ended the sermon. And of course he or more correctly the Tenerife Family Church were in on the project.

13 CONFESSION

Music: Comin' Home Baby – Booker T & the MG's

The Soul Fathers walked back to The Soul Wagon and sat there for a while absorbing all the new information that they had acquired. Lorenzo's heart was heavy in the knowledge that he'd been responsible for the death of Martina.

"You very sad Lorenzo for Martina?"

"I have a confession."

"What is a confession?"

"It was me that started the fire."

"Where?"

"At the casino."

"Why you do this start the fire?"

"I don't know?"

"You don't know why you start the fire? Are you fucking stupid you fucking stupid c@@t?"

Tom was getting angry Lorenzo could tell and he'd never seen Tom angry. He noticed also that Tom's English language skills were improving and he no longer talked in rap speak.

"I honestly don't know why I did it. I think I was making a statement. Something subconscious. Maybe it was something deeper more sinister. Maybe I am really crazy. Maybe it was something to do with me being rescued as a baby from a house fire. We lived above a pizzeria. My parents both died."

"In my time, anybody cannot explain why they do something evil like this then we end the life before the expiry date. Everybody conditioned properly in manufacturing process."

"In the same way that they will end your life?" Lorenzo observed.

"Cardinal #BLi55 will come to make a trial of judgment first," he replied confidently.

"A Cardinal? You mean a religious person?"

"No the cardinal is just the local controller maybe you be calling him big boss? Quite similar to Lager Bob."

"But surely you are guilty of killing the deputy. You admitted it yourself."

"He needs to prove that with the evidence. I did not kill the deputy I only hit him."

"And the saxophone?"

"I can give this back. As you say we can find another one here. It's not so special to me. I have played it now. It plays super brilliant. I do not need to have this particular one."

 Lorenzo's heart was heavy with guilt. It seemed there were two killers on the run dressed as clerics.

 Lorenzo looked in the cracked rear-view mirror and saw

several Neil Diamonds spill out of three black Hummers. He hit the gas after several turns of the ignition and The Soul Wagon spluttered off in a cloud of black exhaust fumes. The smell of burning oil inside the car mixed with the smell of piss and the smell of Pancho was overwhelming. Big hairy dogs sweat heavily in the heat. His big brown eyes smiled at Lorenzo in the rear-view mirror and Lorenzo was pleased to be with his best friend again.

They headed back along the TF-1 in the direction of Las Americas. It didn't take long for the three black Hummers to catch up. Lorenzo took the turning for Los Cristianos and some winding narrow roads that would prevent the Hummers from getting in front of them. Once they got ahead they could block the way. Lorenzo wasn't sure what they wanted but he didn't want to find out. He guessed that they were still working for The Babushka and he guessed they were after him for burning down the house.

Lorenzo cut up the traffic at the big roundabout and drove through the police roadblock that had been set up to check car papers. Two police motorcycles soon joined the chase.

They went down a narrow lane towards the port and one of the Hummers knocked both motorcyclists over. Lorenzo was sort of pleased to see an explosion and a cloud of smoke. But he hoped the police were uninjured, as he didn't need this on his conscience or his criminal record.

They lost the Hummers soon after they drove down a very narrow alley lined with washing hanging between the buildings. Lorenzo soon recognized that they were getting near The Duke of Wellington and there was Lager Bob's big black Merc ahead. He parked behind it but Tom was having one of his fits. It was a particularly bad one.

As soon as they stopped, Tom opened the car door and fell out into the road writhing in agony.

Lorenzo got out to help him and felt himself go dizzy. Somebody had hit him from behind.

Lorenzo hadn't realized that the black Merc S500 he had parked next to was owned by The Babushka. She had been parked nearby The Duke of Wellington waiting for them to arrive.

Tom woke close to midnight and lay in the doorway where he had crawled. He had aged considerably and his hair had grown very long and white and his beard was similarly matching. He looked like an ancient druid.

He composed his thoughts and recalled what had happened. The old Fiat 500 was still there unlocked with headlights on. But there was no sign of Lorenzo, Pancho or the saxophone.

Where could they be? Why would they leave him in the street like this? Why would they leave the car unlocked and with headlights on? His mind was full of questions.

Tom rolled over and picked up his hat and sunglasses lying nearby. He had difficulty getting to his feet and used the car to assist himself. Dusting himself down he felt his long beard and flowing locks. The only place that he could go was to The Duke of Wellington nearby. He observed that the black Merc was no longer parked nearby.

The bar was very busy when he arrived and there was an AC/DC tribute band playing Thunderstruck as he entered. It was deafening but there were many people dancing including the ubiquitous hen parties of screaming women with horny devil headdresses. These lady devils eyed him with disgust.

He approached the bar but Lager Bob didn't recognize him. He roared "OUT" and added "we don't allow paraffins in here" meaning that tramps were not favoured as clientele in his bar.

"It's me Tom Perignon," Tom roared above the noise.

"I don't care what you are collecting for mate, get the fuck out of my pub."

Tom left the noise and stood out in the street. He'd go and sleep in The Soul Wagon and then go talk again with Lager Bob in the morning.

14 THE ULTIMATUM

Music: Uptight Everything's Alright – Stevie Wonder

Lorenzo woke with a thumping headache. His eyesight was blurred. He couldn't rub his head because his hands were tied behind his back but he could feel the lump on his head throb. He wondered if his hat had been damaged and then he realized that Pancho was alone with Tom who was lying unconscious in the street.

He could sense the movement of a boat in harbour and hear the lapping of the water against a fibreglass hull and guessed he was afloat. It was impossible to see in the pitch dark. Lorenzo guessed it must be night-time. He also guessed he'd been kidnapped. Who would kidnap him and why?

"Pancho," he whispered when he smelled the doggy smell.

He didn't want to call out loud in case it would alert unwanted attention. The dog was not in the same room. He could hear Pancho whimper outside and scratch at what may have been a door. Pancho's noises went on for some time and then stopped.

He made a soft sound and Pancho whimpered again. If his

dog had been harmed somebody would have to answer to him. But then his heart became heavy with the knowledge that he'd been responsible for killing somebody's sister and daughter and he wondered why he had a passion for fire.

He lay contemplating this for several hours until the rising sun cast its golden rays through the gaps in the cabin door and through the small porthole windows of the cabin. He needed a piss and he was thirsty at the same time.

Otherwise it was quite tranquil lying on the boat and it was the first time in several days he'd had a bed to sleep on.

After some time he heard footsteps and what he took to be Russian voices and then the movement of the boat as several people stepped aboard. They were all males except one. He wasn't sure what type of boat it was. He doubted if it was a sailing boat most likely a speedboat. The Russian Mafia doesn't do things by half. So it was most likely a hugely powerful and expensive speedboat.

Somebody fumbled with the lock and the padlock was removed. Light filled the small cabin and he saw the giant fat faces of two giant fat faced men who ordered him in broken English to get up.

The tall Russian woman whom he recognized as The Babushka from the casino barked orders at them in Russian. He hoped that she was telling them not to hurt him.

He was unable to do as he was ordered and if he rolled onto his side he would surely have fallen on the floor. Pancho let out a bark but The Babushka seemed to have a way with dogs and she placated him. This was a good sign he hoped.

One of the Russian giants came into the small cabin and pulled him up, spun him round and passed him to giant number two who pulled him on deck. He was escorted to the wheelhouse where The Babushka sat smoking elegantly on her cigarette.

Pancho lay on the floor and eyed him quietly with his big brown eyes.

"Please take a seat Meester Peeterfool," she said as if she was taking another lungful of nicotine.

He was pushed into a canvas chair. It hurt him as his hands were still tied tightly behind his back with a plastic cable grip. The Babushka noticed his discomfort.

"Please release Meester Peeterfool, Maximus," she directed one of her henchmen. He was pulled out of the chair and the plastic ties were cut.

"Please call me Father Lorenzo." He declined to correct her with the pronunciation of his family name.

"You are no more a cleric than I am Yakaterina ze Great. Please take a seat again Lorenzo."

He sat down to wait for further interrogation and flexed his hand to get the blood flowing again. He leant over to stroke Pancho but Pancho seemed frightened to move and lay with his jaw on the floor eying the scene with his big brown eyes.

He looked out over her shoulder behind The Babushka and could see they were in the harbour at Puerto Colon. As he quickly glanced around he realized he was on a giant Rigid Inflatable Boat. He'd heard about this boat. The biggest and fastest RIB in Tenerife. There were only ten of them dotted around the world.

"You want the saxophone?"

"Vaat?"

He ignored her reply.

"Or is it about the fire?"

"Vee see you in security camera. Vee know you start zees fire."

He took a long breath and waited for the interrogation to continue.

"Actually you help me lots. Your friend also not cleric. Your friend Tom Perignon he bust the house. You tried but he was successful. The fire saved me from bankruptcy you see."

Lorenzo explained about the Glitter Gang and the 'Probability App' that had helped him. But The Babushka knew all about that. What she was interested in was how Tom Perignon had managed to do the same thing without any obvious assistance.

"You'll need to ask him yourself because honestly I don't know."

"I would love to do that but he wasn't with you when you parked next to us. Where can we find him?"

Clearly they had not noticed Tom having an ageing fit or whatever they may be called. He explained to her their plans for a benefit concert and cryptocurrency to help the homeless minimum-wage workers in Tenerife.

"Very philanthropic of you but honestly I am more interested in Meester Perignon's skills in calculating probabilities. This will be more useful to me."

He wasn't sure if he should explain that Tom was from the future and that he had a much more interesting skill set than simply beating the house at roulette. He doubted if she would believe him anyway.

"I am very sorry about the fatality. She was a friend of yours I believe. The police have explained everything. You want that I turn you and your friend over to the police so that you can go back to the mental institution where you belong?"

Lorenzo was starting to wonder if that might not be a better option. Things were starting to get out of hand. However he wondered if he might get charged for murder. It seemed likely as there was a fatality and there was evidence of him starting the fire. Who was this Tom Perignon nutcase anyway that had been the catalyst in this catalogue of disasters?

There didn't seem any way out of this mess and so he informed his host that Tom might be found at The Duke of Wellington and that she should ask for him there. Lager Bob their manager would surely assist because both he and Tom were sleeping rough and had no fixed address and of course they were under contract to him.

They gave Lorenzo a drink of water, let him use the bathroom and then put him back below decks amongst the bags of white powder that had recently been placed there. He wasn't sure if Pancho had been left on board or not but he couldn't hear him and he called for him several times.

15 CRY FOR HELP

Music: I Know You Got Soul – James Brown

"I told you last night we don't want paraffins in the bar now fuck off will you mate."

"But Lager Bob it's me Tom Perignon the sax player from The Soul Fathers."

"Out now. You want me to get you some help?"

"Fucks sake you old c@@t it's me, Tom. I've met with an accident." An accident was the only word I could think of that fitted the circumstances. These people were not of an intellectual sophistication to understand.

"Boys." Lager Bob called for help and in the back door piled ten Hell's Angels who stood with arms folded across their chest.

"Your vocabulary is improving son. What's fucking happened to you?" Lager Bob seemed to have experienced a sudden epiphany.

"I tried to explain last time."

"Try me again, I think I was a bit stressed last time," confessed Lager Bob.

So I sat down and went through the whole story again.

"DropDead@40.gene. How the fuck does that work?"

"It's related to the average number of heartbeats in one day. It's built into a genetic timer in my DNA."

"And your partner in crime. Where is he?"

This was the bit I couldn't explain.

"So he's gone missing with his dog and your sax? You c@@ts trying to get out of the contract?"

I explained that this was something to do with either the casino fire, the escape from the psychiatric hospital, the stealing of a police helicopter, or Prof. #ELv15 and the murder of his deputy. Lager Bob was quite impressed by our catalogue of misdemeanours and even though he was a little unconvinced by some of them, he agreed to help us out.

He told me I needed to get rid of my priest's cassock, as it was filthy and smelled of piss and burning oil. He found some Hell's Angels clothing that fitted rather well considering I am so tall. I explained to him I couldn't drive a car but had learned to ride a motorcycle and so he got me a loan of a Harley Davidson Fat Boy. I went and had a shower, got changed and went out and took a test ride along the sea front on the bike.

I was a little hungry and pulled into a little Italian restaurant that I had seen. I got off the bike and put it on its side stand, placed the green synthetic snakeskin helmet over the headlamp and put on my black hat and shades. I adjusted my black leather waistcoat and pulled my beard straight and strutted inside to order some pasta and pesto followed by ice-cream. Fortunately Lager Bob had given me a small impress to assist with any incidental expenditure such as fuel for the bike or pasta and pesto or beer.

The waitress came to take my order. Being very cool I didn't look up from my menu but I did recognize the sweet Czech voice.

"Martina I thought you had," I wasn't allowed to finish.

She looked at me quizzically. Obviously she didn't recognize me without my priestly attire. And of course I looked much older than before, with long white hair and a ZZ Top beard. She had dyed her hair blue although she still had the same blunt cut bob that she had at the casino. She had dyed her hair blue I presume, to look less conspicuous.

"Sister Martina it's me Tom. Tom Perignon," I used the title sister so that she knew that I knew her from the penitentiary psychiatric ward.

Her face lit up with that pleasing smile that she used to flirt with. Her mouth pouted with temptation. Those were the lips I wanted to kiss and that was the tongue I wanted to taste. I looked at her closely. She was ripe and edible and she had no signs of burns.

She still hadn't said a word.

"You survived the fire?"

"Can I take your order sir?" she asked curtly.

"Martina Topolova, it's you isn't it?"

"I think you are mistaking me for another friend of yours sir," she lied sexily in her Czech accented English.

I asked her in Czech why she was reported missing after the fire at the casino. She ignored what I had said.

"So you would like spaghetti with green pesto," she fore-guessed my order in English, turned and walked away. I studied her form carefully. It was fantastic and I knew it was Martina for sure.

My food came but was delivered by a different waitress. I ate in silence only sipping beer for company. I called for my bill, paid at the checkout, went outside and leant on the bike.

I had a premonition that she would come eventually and so I waited patiently for thirty long minutes. But she didn't arrive and so I put on my helmet and started the bike. As I was moving off I felt a hand on my shoulder and caught a glimpse of Martina as she slipped behind me onto the rear mudguard rubbing my back with her magnificent chest as she did so.

There is no pillion seat on the Fat Boy so I rode only a hundred meters down the road into another parking slot where we could have a discrete chat.

The casino fire had ended the Topolova Twins' lucrative gigs there and so Martina's brother had decided on an insurance claim so that they could go to America to pursue their careers. I reminded her that she was perpetrating an insurance fraud and she said she had no other options. She didn't consider waitressing a long-term career move.

I explained what had happened to Lorenzo and she said she would help as much as she could. She'd make some enquiries of The Babushka. I reminded her that The Babushka thought she was dead. She reminded me that The Babushka was Russian and would understand her predicament.

I spun the bike round with a quick burst of the throttle and took her back to the restaurant as she'd only stopped for a rest break. Now I now knew where to find her.

I rode back to The Duke of Wellington feeling rather pleased with myself. However the thing about rapid ageing and I must confess I have very little experience with normal ageing, is that you notice dramatic changes in your abilities. For example I now need to pee a lot, my eyesight isn't so good and neither is my balance. Overall my reactions are a little slower. Being aware of this is a key stage in them not becoming a hindrance I guess. But every cloud has a silver lining and I found that my perceptions were also now a little different.

I parked the Fat Boy with the other bikes behind The Duke and went inside. Lager Bob and daughter Rita were having a meeting with a group of Elvis Presley tribute singers. Lager Bob welcomed me by calling me David and asked me to sit at the back. Prof. #ELv15 had been there for some time threatening Lager Bob with more Karaoke. I'm not sure what else he could use as a threat.

Lager Bob told them that he'd seen the saxophone in the possession of #TMp319 and if he came upon the saxophone he would make sure that they had their rightful property returned to them. He also told them that if they felt justice had to be done in respect of the yet to be committed future murder, then surely a trial was necessary. The important point he emphasized was that the murder was in the future and the victim wasn't even born yet. I guess Prof. #ELv15 hadn't thought of that. So any trial needed to take place after the crime.

Prof. #ELv15 reluctantly agreed to a trial and said he would return with Cardinal #BLi55 the chief adjudicator. Lager Bob reiterated that any trial had to be after the murders had taken place and therefore in the future. Prof. #ELv15 acknowledged this but highlighted that when they got a hold of #TMp319 he would need to be extradited back to the future so that a trial could take place. Lager Bob pointed out that there were no grounds for extradition because no crime had been committed yet. Prof. #ELv15 said that the theft of the saxophone was a crime. Even though the theft took place in the future and that #TMp319 was known to have been in possession of the sax and Lager Bob had acknowledged that fact. Lager Bob was happy to concede that technicality.

There was a young woman sitting next to Prof. #ELv15.

She was my life-partner #MTn469 and she had not been affected by rapid ageing and so I assumed she had only just arrived here. She is the same age as I am and like all females she is fitted with dropDead@33.gene and I wasn't sure if she would survive rapid ageing as well as or better than I had done. But clearly we both needed to get back to our own time to find out if rapid ageing could be reversed. I know that the alleged murder would be committed in the future and so I would most likely face a future trial.

I suppressed my telepathic communications which is how we normally interact with each other, because I didn't want Prof. #ELv15 to know I was in the room. He and his assistants hadn't recognized me and #MTn469 either hadn't recognised me or had pretended not to. I guessed the latter.

Seeing #MTn469 reminded me that I love her, so why had I had such strong feelings for the now allegedly deceased Martina? Are all women exactly the same? These two were identical except they are in different stages of the ageing process and from different epochs. Maybe their experiences set them apart? Martina Topolova had been an acrobat with about thirty years of life behind her and #MTn469 is a laboratory technician with about three years of life behind her. Is it possible to be in love with two women at the same time?

After the Elvis gang left us, Lager Bob pointed out that obviously the sax was with The Babushka or the police and I should try to get it back so it could be returned to its rightful owners. He thought the chances of the police having it were nil. And so he deduced that I should talk with The Babushka.

"Who's the cute blonde they had with them? She's obviously not an Elvis tribute," Lager Bob quizzed.

"She's my wife from the future and interestingly she has not aged so I guess she's just arrived." I used the word wife but we actually use the term life-partner and I knew that rapid ageing would set in soon. I wasn't sure if Prof. #ELv15's gang were immune to the rapid ageing or they had found a way to avoid it perhaps by only coming to this time for a few hours at a time.

"She looks familiar," Lager Bob pointed out.

"This is quite bizarre, she looks like a younger version of Martina Topolova the acrobat from the casino. You know the one who got killed in the fire." I feigned the truth.

"Well if you could get her looking a bit older you might get Lorenzo off the hook for murder. I'm sure they will throw the book at him if they catch him."

This was quite a genius observation I thought and if we got the timing right it might be possible.

16 LOOKING FOR LORENZO

Music: Love City – Sly & the Family Stone

The following day I decided to take a ride to the Buddhist monastery to find Victoria the guitarist and her band. I planned later to go and eat pasta and pesto and talk with Martina with the expectation that I could get a lead to find Lorenzo. After this I'd head back to The Duke as I was also hoping that the extradition trial would take place soon because I didn't want #MTn469 to suffer unduly. I guess that this was exactly the reason they brought her so as to put pressure on me.

It was another typically hot autumn Canarian day with a huge build-up of heavy cloud over El Teide. There would most likely be more rain up in the high ground and the mountain was looking a little bit greener every day. However the monastery was near Playa Paraiso about thirty minutes ride away down by the sea.

I love the freedom of motorcycling and feeling the wind in my beard and the cooling breeze. This is better than the simulator, maybe because I have a beard, maybe because it is not a simulation.

The monastery doesn't look like such. In fact it looks like a regular finca or farmhouse, which is exactly what it is. I parked the bike in the forecourt and strolled inside to ask for sister Victoria guessing that she would also be referred to as sister.

Inside the building I could hear quite audibly the sounds of a three-piece rock band belting out Sunshine of Your Love, the old Cream hit from 1960s. I followed the noise to an upstairs room where three orange clad musicians were rehearsing.

I introduced myself and explained The Soul Fathers project. I received an enthusiastic response to our ambitions to help the homeless minimum-wage workers in Tenerife. Their guru had recently died and they felt that this could be a fitting tribute in his memory. I decided they didn't need to know about The Church for Everyday People as Lager Bob had decided to call it. The people of the Twenty First Century still need labels to hang on things and so I hoped to eliminate any confusion or problems.

I explained that two people fronted The Soul Fathers and my partner Lorenzo had been having some trouble with a Russian casino owner. Victoria surprised me by telling me that The Babushka had previously been living here at the monastery for a while using the rehabilitation facility and that she had two sons who helped her run her business empire. She was saddened to hear that the Joy casino had recently burned down.

Victoria and her band agreed to come for a meeting to The Duke of Wellington to discuss rehearsals and the eventual concert. I couldn't really do anything without Lorenzo but I hoped he'd turn up before the meeting. I left to go eat pasta and pesto and hopefully meet with Martina.

My feelings about Martina were a little confused as I didn't really know her well. She looked identical although older than #MTn469. Was I attracted by her looks or by the true essence of the person? #MTn469 had been appointed as my life-partner ever since we were hatched, so a little over three years. I wonder if Martina has the same flaws as my #MTn469? My mind seemed to be constantly running a comparison competition.

I jumped on the bike and headed back to Las Americas. On joining the motorway I saw ahead a convoy of three black Hummers and so I sat well behind to see where they were heading. The convoy took the turning for Puerto Colon and I followed them discreetly at a distance. I doubt if they would recognize me but it made sense to not draw attention to myself on an orange Harley Davidson.

The convoy headed to the port and went through the security barrier. I decided to park up this side of the quay so as to see what was happening at a distance. It was very busy with holidaymakers and workers and van deliveries but I found an unobtrusive spot to park the bike.

One of the Neil Diamonds got out of the front passenger door of the middle Hummer and opened the rear passenger door. Out stepped The Babushka puffing smoke into the air from a cigarette and looking very elegant. And then out jumped Pancho behind her on a lead. There was no sign of Lorenzo. Two very tall men who were not dressed as Neil Diamonds simultaneously got out of the front car. I took these to be The Babushka's sons and one of them I recognized to be the manager at the now defunct casino. The sons and mother boarded a large speedboat. It looked large enough to live aboard and so I guessed that's where Lorenzo and the sax would be. I'd go and take a look when they'd gone.

I waited by the bike for over one hour but the phone in my pocket rang. Lager Bob had given me a mobile phone and said he'd call me if the extradition trial was going to happen. I answered the phone and it was as expected. He said there was a comedy Elvis and a bishop waiting for me which I took to mean Prof. #ELv15 and Cardinal #BLi55 were at the Duke of Wellington. I fired up the bike and headed back.

17 TRIAL

Music: Where Is The Love – Donny Hathaway & Roberta Flack

Lager Bob and Rita were sitting at the big round table on the terrace in the shade. Sitting with them was Prof. #ELv15 and the huge bloated personality of Cardinal #BLi55 plus #MTn469. The rest of the Elvis gang was nowhere to be seen.

I kissed #MTn469 and said hello to the others. She was shocked by my appearance and initially she didn't know who I was. She hadn't aged so I assumed they had not stayed here overnight.

"Can you explain why I am ageing so fast?" I immediately directed the question at Prof. #ELv15 and Cardinal #BLi55 as I took a seat next to Lager Bob opposite my #MTn469.

"It's quite simple. The dropDead@40.gene is the problem. It controls your ageing but because the Network is not active here, the gene is out of control," answered the Cardinal.

"Network?" asked Lager Bob and Rita in unison.

"Think of it like a public Wi-Fi. In our future time, everything is run across the Network. We have another name for it but you understand this concept I am sure," explained the Cardinal.

"Listen I don't have the sax. Not anymore. It's been stolen." I thought I'd drop that in before Lager Bob and Rita started to draw a comparison with the Matrix movie and hijack the conversation. I wanted to get this over and done with as quickly as possible.

"A small detail which we can address forthwith," replied Prof. #ELv15.

"So does anyone dispute my authority here?" asked Cardinal #BLi55.

Nobody spoke up.

"Let me recap then. There has been a murder of the deputy at the campus."

"There will be a murder. It has not happened yet," Lager Bob, stressed the word 'will' as he offered a defense.

"Yes this is true. It is true in this time but in the future these things have already happened."

"And so a trial can only take place in the future after the event has happened because there has not yet been a crime," demanded Lager Bob using the logic he had developed previously.

"And therefore we can request extradition of the suspect," suggested the Cardinal.

Lager Bob seemed to be assuming the role as my defence lawyer, and so he asked the obvious question, "Who is the accused and what is the evidence?"

"#TMp319 is the accused and we do have video evidence of him," answered the Cardinal.

I was about to speak because I was confused about attempted

rather than actual murder, but Lager Bob told me to shut up and save it for the main trial. He went on to ask, "You want me to extradite somebody for a crime that has not been committed yet?"

"Well there is also the crime of theft. Theft of the saxophone. And we also have video evidence of that too."

The local police arrived and interrupted things. Rita got up and spoke to them in Spanish and took them inside. I felt a little tense but was sure that they wouldn't recognize me now.

"Bloody police. Every fucking week they come. Want to shut me down. Tell me my papers are not in order. Guy my partner sorts it out with them. It will only take a moment."

Lager Bob remained silent until the two officers came out. They nodded at him and left carrying a brown paper bag.

"I think we are clear about the sax being in the accused's possession. The point I would make is who is the rightful owner?" Lager Bob's defense skills were quite well developed.

"It is owned by the Campus museum," said the Cardinal indignantly.

"That would be subject to some debate and evidence. It's possible that the campus museum is in possession of misappropriated goods. Look at the Elgin Marbles in the British Museum for an example of what I am talking about."

"#TMp319 needs to come with us to be questioned and tried and the saxophone needs to be returned. If he doesn't come with us then he can stay here and die, and his life-partner with him. She will soon become afflicted by the rapid ageing that you have seen on #TMp319."

I interrupted the Cardinal. "How can you prevent me from coming back?"

"We will change the location of the portals. Then you will not be able to find them and use them. Quite simple and effective really."

#MTn469 confirmed that they could do this as she had seen it done already. She didn't have the same Czech accented English as her Twenty First Century doppelgänger. "I want to be with you," she demanded meekly.

"I'd love for you to have the sax. Here it's not the last saxophone in existence. There are plenty more here."

"Are you coming with us or are you staying here in the Twenty First Century?" demanded Cardinal #BLi55.

"We are staying here," #MTn469 called out angrily.

The Cardinal looked at me and I nodded in agreement.

"Very well then we will leave you to your own devices. We will come back and check on you from time to time. Hopefully you will be able to return the saxophone," the Cardinal said as he and Prof. #ELv15 stood to leave. Lager Bob stood to shake hands but they dismissed us all and turned and left. They walked off in the direction of the nearby shopping center.

"How did you get here?" I asked #MTn469 as I looked into her beautiful blue eyes.

"A portal opened up in the shopping center nearby. It was only a short walk. And you?"

"I came through a portal in the base of a pyramid at Guïmar."

"Guïmar?"

"Guïmar is a small town to the north of here. We are on an island called Tenerife."

"Tenerife? We are not on Campus?"

"This is an island close to the coast of Africa."

"Does not matter. All the time portals that you know of will be closed off by now."

We both realized that we had been communicating without telepathy. She had a sweet high-pitched voice. I'd never heard her speak before. I loved the sound of her voice.

"So we are here on the Devil's Island. The local people, the Guanches say that El Teide was the prison of Guyaota." She then added "The Devil," for clarity.

"Grouchos?" asked Lager Bob but Rita corrected him.

Rita asked us if we were hungry, but #MTn469 did not understand this concept and so I explained about food.

Rita explained the menu and #MTn469 was keen to try the chocolate cheesecake and so Rita brought her a portion with ice cream.

"Wait till you try pasta and pesto and also beer."

I let her taste some of my pasta and pesto and she was equally enthusiastic but a little bloated. I explained that Lorenzo also liked pasta and pesto and also he loved beer. But of course she didn't know anything about Lorenzo or The Soul Fathers or about The Church of Everyday People or the benefits concert or cryptocurrency. And so I went through the story right from the start.

Lager Bob and Rita sat listening intently and clearly there were some parts of the story that they were unfamiliar with. After some time they were all up to speed with what was happening.

"We better go and get Lorenzo," suggested Lager Bob.

"I'll get you your bill," said Rita and returned immediately with the slip of paper and put it in front of #MTn469 as she knew my expenses were covered by the contract for The Soul Fathers.

#MTn469 looked at the bill quizzically.

"It's a request for an amount of money. They call it a factura," I told her. Then I directed my conversation at Lager Bob and his daughter. "We don't use money in the future she doesn't have any money. Doesn't know what it is."

Rita was about to explain about charity but her father stopped her. "Leave it love, put it in the book for The Soul Fathers will you." He sounded unusually apologetic.

#MTn469 complained of feeling unwell and I realized she had never consumed this type of meal before and so I helped her to get to the bathroom.

As she got up from the table she had an ageing fit in front of everybody. Now Lager Bob and Rita could see our predicament and were visibly shocked. She writhed in agony on the floor in spasms for several minutes and I lay beside her and held her tight. I really felt for her because I knew what she was going through and I knew what the eventual outcome was likely to be if we didn't do something about it and I didn't know how much time we had.

18 RECOVERING LORENZO

Music: He's Misstra Know It All – Stevie Wonder

#MTn469 was a mess and Rita brought her some clothes because her orange boiler suit had become soiled. She took a shower and got changed. #MTn469 liked the new clothes and admired herself in the big mirror on the wall inside. She had aged noticeably and looked about the same age as Martina.

Now looking super sexy in pink pedal pusher pants and a black leather jacket and with long blond hair #MTn469 and Martina Topolova could have been twin sisters although Martina now had blue hair cut into a blunt bob.

I had an idea. I asked Rita to cut #MTn469's hair. Once this was completed Guy came to pick us up in the black Mercedes and we headed to Puerto Colon.

We sat in the back with Lager Bob and Rita sat in the front passenger seat. #MTn469 wanted to know how frequently the ageing fits occurred. I had not noticed any pattern and pointed out that for her it would most likely be different.

"You just let me handle this son when we get there," ordered Lager Bob.

Guy remained silent in the driving seat. I recognised him as the man who stood at the bar in The Duke of Wellington wearing snakeskin Cuban heeled boots drinking tequila most of the day.

When we arrived at the harbour we drove directly through the barrier after taking a ticket. I directed Guy to the quayside where the big flashy speedboat was moored and where I thought Lorenzo might be. We parked the big Merc not too close to the boat so as to not attract suspicion. Lager Bob and I exited the vehicle and the ladies and driver stayed put.

"Nobody about?" said Lager Bob.

He meant nobody on the boat but there were other people around. It was early evening in a busy harbour after all.

We stepped aboard and saw that there was a padlock holding the cabin door closed. Lager Bob produced a crowbar from inside his checked jacket and unceremoniously forced the door open with a crunch.

Staring up at us gagged and bound was Lorenzo still dressed in his clerical robes. I could see he had lost his crucifix. I climbed into the cabin and released him from his bondage. He looked at me suspiciously.

"It's me," I croaked. My voice had obviously changed because he still didn't recognize me and of course it was dark.

"Come on son, up you get," whispered Lager Bob and I helped Lorenzo out onto the dark deck. Lorenzo complied and obviously recognized Lager Bob. I handed Lorenzo his hat and sunglasses and that's when he recognized me.

"Jesus Christ man what the actual fuck has happened to you?"

I hadn't known Lorenzo a long time but I had never heard him express surprise like that before.

"Lets get a shift on," ordered Lager Bob who was concerned that we might get interrupted. And so we disembarked and walked back to the car. The S500 Mercedes is a big and spacious vehicle but not enough room for four on the back seat with comfort and so #MTn469 got out.

Lorenzo gave her a big smile and went to kiss her on the cheek when I introduced her as my wife.

"Your wife? You got married? Holy guacamole."

"No, my wife from the future. I'll explain later."

"But she's." I interrupted Lorenzo and confirmed she looks identical to Martina although I didn't mention the lack of tattoos.

"I can find my own way back," offered Guy in the driver seat.

"No don't worry Guy we can manage," said Lager Bob cheerily. I was to observe that he never referred to Guy by any other name.

"Luckily Pancho isn't here otherwise what would we do?" observed Lorenzo as #MTn469 sat on my lap with Lager Bob in the middle.

Lager Bob grunted at the inconvenience.

"Where is he?" asked Lorenzo.

"I think he maybe with The Babushka?" answered Guy.

"How do you know?" I demanded.

"Because that is her boat."

"You know her?" I asked.

"Of course."

I decided not to enquire further until I'd sussed him out. We headed back to The Duke of Wellington in silence. For some reason I felt compelled not to mention the saxophone and fortunately nobody else did either.

Guy parked the car outside The Duke and got out and opened the door for us. He was as tall as I am and dark skinned with a shaved head. He was covered in tattoos including tattoos on his dark face and head. Beside his bright blue eyes that shone like beacons were two giant golden earrings that made him look like a pirate. He left us to go back into the kitchen. But before he left he shook hands with Lorenzo and whispered something in his ear.

"What did he say?" I was curious to know.

"Something about being pleased to meet a man who appreciates the power of fire." And as an afterthought he told me that Guy's breath stank of farts.

"Why did The Babushka capture you?" I'd been dying to ask Lorenzo and hoped that he had an answer.

"She wants to know how you were able to calculate probabilities and beat the house without any assistance."

"I do not know. It is just something I can do."

"She won't like that answer. You better come up with something so that you can get your sax back." And then Lorenzo added as an afterthought "And Pancho too."

"She could have asked me or captured me."

"You were having one of those fits. She didn't recognize you, remember?"

Rita came out and told us that Guy was going to cook something special for us tonight and so we should hang around.

19 BACK AT THE PESTO RESTAURANT

Music: Watch Out Girl - The Embers

We sat down at the table set with silver and other finery. It would seem this was a special occasion but it was not. Guy always entertained extravagantly apparently. I brought Lorenzo up to speed with the situation regarding the sax needing to go back to the future otherwise #MTn469 and I couldn't return and also told him that I'd met Martina working in an Italian restaurant.

Lorenzo was relieved that she hadn't died in the fire and was amused that she and her brother were involved in insurance fraud. He briefly discussed the question of how he could get off the hook for murder without getting her into trouble but I pointed out that it was her brother's problem.

Guy had joined us for dinner and had brought a bottle of tequila. He was a very quiet and reserved man but he more than made up for this with his tattooed appearance and his drinking habits, which required neither salt nor lemon. He sat opposite me but even at that distance I knew what Lorenzo meant about his halitosis. He'd prepared some exceptionally spicy chicken wings and a variety of Mexican style tapas. Guy had heard snippets of our story but we didn't know much about him. It was as if he'd read our minds and he opened the conversation.

"Please allow me to introduce myself. I am a man of wealth and taste. Pleased to meet you. And what's puzzling you is the nature of my game."

His words seemed strangely familiar. Lorenzo muttered under his breath something about Rolling Stones lyrics. Eventually we got the full dialogue from Guy about his life so far. I'm sure he only told us half the story. The bits that he wanted us to hear. It's not unusual.

The nature of his game was that he was involved in many projects in USA and in Tenerife. I guess he'd had projects in other places too but those were the ones he focused on. I wondered if he was Guy the agent that the Neil Diamond tribute singer referred to when we first played in the hotel a few days ago?

He told us that the cryptocurrency was a good idea but that it needed to have some real substance behind it and suggested that it should be asset-backed. Obviously Lager Bob had been sharing our ideas with his business partner.

Guy thought that a rare mineral would be the best substance. I suggested gold but his knowledge of minerals was impressive and he told us that silver was rarer than gold. He couldn't understand the human obsession with gold because as an element it was quite abundant on Earth.

He suggested coltan, which is industrially known as tantalite and is used in the manufacture of electric cars and other appliances and batteries. He said coltan could be traded on lightly regulated stock exchanges around the world. His premise was that demand would soon outstrip supply and the price and profits would go through the roof. He also advised us that tantalite could be recycled but that it was cheaper to mine it with a subdued and compliant workforce. In order to keep control of the price we should also be in control of recycling. He seemed to be a shrewd businessman but without any concern for the environment or for the planet.

Lorenzo wanted to meet with Martina but The Soul Wagon wasn't suitable for the three of us and smelled of piss so Guy offered to drive us over there. Guy also wanted to meet somebody who had cheated death by fire. Lager Bob and Rita stayed behind as they'd taken pity on Neil Diamond and asked one of his tribute acts back tonight for a gig.

Again #MTn469 and I sat in the back and Lorenzo in his cassock was up front with Tequila Guy. Lager Bob had offered to get him a change of clothes but Lorenzo was comfortable with his image even if it meant a possible run in with the cops.

My stomach was uneasy due to the spicy food and as soon as we pulled up outside the restaurant I rushed straight inside for the toilets. Immediately I took another ageing fit but this one was the worst I'd ever had and by the time the spasms had finished I found Lorenzo standing over me. I could feel his presence but I couldn't see him because I had gone totally blind. He spoke to me but I could tell from his voice he was shaken by what he saw. I couldn't see and he said my eyes were blank and just staring ahead into space. Perhaps I'd had some sort of stroke. As Lorenzo had told me previously, old age is not a disease.

He helped me up but I felt very frail. He handed me my hat and sunglasses and I steadied myself to put them on and we went out of the bathroom and struggled slowly to the table where the others were watching and waiting. The silence from them was deafening and I could tell everybody was really shocked by my appearance. I took off my sunglasses as a silent way of explaining further and #MTn469 started to sob. She got up to assist me into the seat. There was no need for her to ask me what had happened because she instinctively knew and told me that I needed to get the sax back and give it to Prof. #ELv15 and Cardinal #BLi55 so we could go home.

Martina was just finishing her shift when she walked through the restaurant. It was Lorenzo who called her over. They chatted but I couldn't hear them very well.

I sensed Guy had arrived and this was confirmed by the dreadful odour of sulphur. I think he must have been standing close to me. He'd been outside parking the car. The S500 is a big beast and needs a lot of space. Finding somewhere to park in the hotspots of Tenerife is becoming increasingly more difficult on a daily basis it would seem.

#MTn469 confirmed later to me that there had been an instant mutual attraction between Guy and Martina and it seemed to really shock Lorenzo. I know he has a thing for Martina so it's understandable. Seemingly her proud breasts and tattoo were on display for all the world to see.

There was room in the car for one more and due to my condition they didn't want to stay and so we went straight back to The Duke of Wellington and spent another hour trying to find a parking space nearby. Martina sat in the front passenger seat and I could feel Lorenzo's anger as he sat next to me.

"Where are you staying tonight?" asked Martina talking over her shoulder.

It was a good question. I assumed we would be back on the beach. Lorenzo had assumed I think that he would be sharing a bed with Martina. I'm not sure what Guy assumed. His assumptions were unimportant because Martina had assumed she would be spending the night with Guy. That much was obvious even to me sitting blind in the back of the car.

The kitchen was closed and Guy was free to roam as he pleased until breakfast time tomorrow morning.

#MTn469 helped me out of the car. I'm not sure how Martina could spend time with a man with such awful halitosis but I suppose love is blind or maybe even anosmic too.

Lorenzo was blind but he was blind with fury. It's common knowledge that all anger is caused by frustration and his frustration was caused by being rejected in favour of Mister stinky mouth. He marched off muttering something about getting drunk.

#MTn469 assisted me into The Duke of Wellington which was really busy because not only was there the celebratory crucifixion of Neil Diamond's fabulous canon of work, there was the weekly darts competition with associated boisterous bacchanalian banter.

The bar was busy and I was a little hungry but the chef had gone off to seduce Martina. I felt pretty old and consequently uninterested in her amorous adventures. I was also disinterested in beer. I was afraid of it too because my bathroom trips were becoming more frequent and my ageing fits if that is what they could be called, seemed to occur at that moment.

We found Lorenzo at the bar but he sank a swift whisky and was just about to leave when I realized I still had my crucifix in my pocket as my cassock was still in the laundry. I doubt if I'd need the religious attire again as it seemed unlikely that I'd be able to play the benefit gig whenever that might be. Lorenzo hung the cross round his neck and bid us good night but I stopped him and asked him to take us to The Soul Wagon and I explained to #MTn469 that we could sleep in it. If we got too uncomfortable or the smell of piss got too much we could always go and sleep on the beach.

As he walked off into the night I reminded him that I had arranged for all the band members to meet in The Duke at 1pm tomorrow.

20 BAND MEETING

Music: Chinese Checkers – Booker T. & the MG's

I felt disinclined to eat breakfast cooked by a man with heinous halitosis and so we went somewhere else to dine. I'm not sure where it was because I was unable to see and #MTn469 doesn't know the area. However we eventually found our way back to The Duke of Wellington in time for the meeting after a casual stroll around town.

It's just as well we ate elsewhere because Guy had failed to turn up for his shift and so the kitchen was still closed. Lager Bob was furious but not as furious as he was when the Casanova chef eventually did arrive. It was the first time I heard him refer to Guy by another name. Several other names screamed at a loud volume actually.

Next to arrive was Lorenzo. I'm not sure how he looked because I couldn't see him. However he confirmed that #MTn469 must have had another ageing fit too, because she seemed more matronly. The night in the car had been uneventful for me and I'd slept well although evidently I'd pissed myself in my sleep. This ageing game is very impractical and somewhat demeaning.

#MTn469 was too obsessed with her hot and cold menopausal sweats to engage in conversation to describe how Lorenzo looked after his night on the tiles.

But Rita came to see how we were. She didn't notice I was blind and I didn't take my sunglasses off, as I didn't need sympathy.

"How long do you think it will take to organize the benefit concert?" I enquired.

"It won't be until after Christmas. Easter is a probably a better target and also Easter is a much more important festival here in Tenerife," she replied.

"So we are going to have a hot cross bun festival," observed Lorenzo. He had to explain to me about the various festivals of Christianity.

Victoria and her bass player and drummer arrived crashing through the main doors with piles of equipment. They had assumed that this would be an audition not just a meeting. They immediately started setting up and neither Lorenzo nor I was prepared to stop them. We just needed the Jet Free Horns, some keyboards and the backing vocals and also a much younger me with a sax to complete the line-up.

Ebony Tony was the next to arrive and his surprise guest was Pancho. Lorenzo was ecstatic with joy and took his dog outside again for a walk. When he returned Lager Bob came over to say that dogs were not allowed in the pub. I must confess I had lost interest in the whole project and so I sat with Pancho on the terrace to contemplate my future.

Sitting outside I listened to Victoria's three-piece band warm up. They were called The Lounge Lizards. Their brand of funky music was good and I drew on my expert knowledge of soul music to think of some songs that we could perform. I guess the plan had to be to go back to the future to rejuvenate and then return for the performance if that was possible. The philanthropic aspects of the project were not as important to me because I was not of this time but the musical performance was of interest.

The smell of sulphur filled the air and I sensed that Guy was approaching.

"May I sit down?" he asked as Pancho grew restless and the sounds of The Isley Brothers' version of Summer Breeze drifted outside towards me.

Victoria's guitar playing was awesome. But of course Summer Breeze was not a soul number in its first incarnation. The song was originally by the rock duo Seals & Croft and was much slower paced. I prefer the Isley Brothers' version I must confess. But it was now my turn to extract a confession. However my mind wandered and I thought what it must be like to live a normal human lifespan and hear music again some fifty years or more later. Would you reminisce? Would a song remind you of that first kiss? I now felt about eighty years old but had only been alive for a few years and even I am wondering where all the time has gone. My daydreaming ceased.

"How did you get on with Martina?" I asked with feigned interest.

"Huh that bitch," was all I could elicit. I felt a little aggrieved at Guy's remarks because I had become very fond of Martina not withstanding her choice in male escorts.

"She has a keen sense," I commented, I withheld the words "of smell." I'm not sure if he understood. I knew that she had a keen sense of balance too but that was out of context of the conversation. I guess Spanish must be his first language and so I tried again in that as I now had assumed some mastery of it.

"If you think Spanish is my first language then you are mistaken," he answered in Guanche the native tongue of Tenerife.

"You don't like the language of the Conquistadores?" I answered in Guanche.

"I am not as old as you think?"

I was starting to get sleepy but the odour of smelling salts filled the air enough to keep me awake.

"Listen I can help you get back to your own time and #MTn469 too. I can help you, if you let me."

He seemed very amiable but I was a little suspicious and I wondered how he could achieve that. I didn't want to prolong the conversation so didn't ask.

"And in return?"

"Martina told me about the sax."

"You want the sax and in return you will help us get back to the future?"

"As you are aware there are plenty of saxophones here."

I was aware of that but wasn't sure if he was. After all it was possible he could have any sax he wanted. He could even have one made.

"It's solid gold," he added.

"Indeed it is. And it used to belong to a President of the United States of America."

He laughed out loud and looked at me. I could smell the odour change direction and it hit me on the face like a wet flannel.

"He used to play the national anthem on it whilst his secretary was performing fellatio on him. Did you know that?"

I didn't know that and said as much. I wondered why a secretary giving attention to an erect president standing to attention might be important to Guy. I think what he was telling me was urban myth.

All metals have a weight ratio to water. Gold is nineteen times denser than water. One liter of water weighs one kilogram so one liter of gold weighs nineteen kilograms. The gold sax is very heavy even for me when I was fit enough to play it, about two and a half times heavier than a normal brass one so around fifteen kilograms. Too heavy to be holding when you are enjoying the carnal delights of having your staff sucked off by your staff.

"Let me have a think about it?" was all I could muster. Maybe he would prefer a platinum sax. Platinum is twenty-one times heavier than water and much more valuable than gold but I expect he knew all of this as he looked like a heavy metal type of guy.

"And get your sidekick to remove that crucifix. Some people find that sort of idolatry offensive," he barked in English.

I gazed dreamily out to sea and saw the sun shimmer on the horizon behind the wind surfers and yachts. But of course this was just my imagination and I dozed off into a deep sleep as the stench of sulphur drifted off in the direction of the kitchen.

"The world will become a better place if you let me have it," he said as he faded out of my life.

Lorenzo woke me from my slumber.

"Fucking awesome those dudes," he shouted excitedly referring to The Lounge Lizards.

"Yes I can tell."

"Was that c@@t out here?" I knew which c@@t he was talking about; I could smell the refreshing scent of his absence. Lorenzo seemed to also have been inflicted with Lager Bob's colourful vocabulary.

I needed to get the sax back immediately and said as much to Lorenzo. We had to find The Babushka as she was the most likely candidate. And we had to find her quickly. Lorenzo didn't want to help me if it involved meeting with Martina and in any case he had his dog back. His life was going on as normal but mine wasn't.

"The world will become a better place if you let me have it," Guy had said. I wonder what he meant by that? I dozed off again to be awoken by a distant argument between a man and a woman that was taking place in the car park. The Czech accented English was familiar.

"But I didn't do anything. What has my life to do with you anyway? Fuck off." It was brutally put but jealousy is the product of desire or maybe the product of love.

21 ACCIDENT WAITING TO HAPPEN

Music: Hold Back The Night - Trammps

Martina had spent an interesting evening doing nothing with Guy at his cave home. He lived up the mountain cum volcano way past the town of Vilaflor near the peak of El Teide. She couldn't remember getting there or leaving, she assumed they went in the Mercedes all she can remember is darkness and then being above the clouds.

She was very confused about the things Guy had told her. He had said that he remembered Christopher Columbus or Cristobal Colon as he called him when he came through here on his way to accidentally discover America some four hundred years ago. He had described how he had advised the adventurer to leave the island before he erupted El Teide. How could Guy possibly erupt El Teide?

He had said the last time that he had caused a summit eruption was about one thousand three hundred years ago but he had made several side vent eruptions just to warn the locals. He had caused the destruction of the main port of Garachico in 1706 with a side vent eruption because the population had wanted to build a cathedral against his wishes. However he had made sure that lava flows had not harmed any religious buildings. He refused to tell why he had caused the earlier summit eruption although Martina thought it was probably something to do with the Vikings who came to the island and who refused to offer him the huge horn that they had sounded as they landed. Guy had talked about the Vikings a lot and about them not having respect.

He had also explained how he had helped shape the economy of Tenerife into the tourist destination that it is now. He had been involved in the creation of holiday resorts and the building of hotels.

Guy's personal traits were that he seemed to like a lot of noise, spicy food and tequila. Martina shared his enthusiasm for tequila. She also shared his enthusiasm for heavy metal music although Guy also had an interest in other styles too. They had sat up all night listening to Black Sabbath, which was his favourite band.

Guy was also a talented musician and although originally a fiddle player he could also play bass and guitar. However his dream was to learn to play saxophone. Even though he'd worked and studied abroad, mostly in the USA, he'd never had time to learn saxophone. Charlie Parker was his favourite but he had recently taken to listening to Maceo Parker and Guy thought they must be a very musical family to have produced such talent. His sax of preference was therefore alto.

Martina had explained that Tom's gold saxophone had gone missing on the island. She wasn't sure if it was an alto or not.

Guy reasoned that if Tom couldn't take care of the sax then somebody else ought to have it and make use of it.

She kept all this information to herself including his full name, which was Guyaota Cabra Follar.

He had also told her "I am El Teide and El Teide is me.

Every time you see El Teide you are looking at me." She wasn't sure she should take that at face value or whether it was some kind of metaphor. She knew from her native Czechia that malevolent spirits called čerts inhabited bogs and springs but these were ancient pagan stories and kids' fairy tales. His bold claim really frightened her. But she liked excitement in her life.

Notwithstanding any of the above she quite liked Guy. He was different and he was interesting and he had copious quantities of tequila.

Lorenzo had a man's intuition and he knew also that she did.

"Did you check the car?"

I was enjoying another senile siesta when Lorenzo interrupted me again. He repeated the question just to make sure I wasn't suffering from dementia.

"Check the car for what?"

"For your sax? Holy guacamole. Have you not looked in the boot?"

Lorenzo was quite agitated. I hadn't looked in the boot. He had a point.

"Gimme the fucking keys you old fool."

I gave him the car keys and he went off. Ten minutes later he returned. I heard him walk up and stand in front of me.

"You silly old fool," he said as he held out the saxophone in its case. I guess that was what he was doing because there was a dull thump as he put it down seconds later. It's very heavy.

"Why the fuck did you not look in the bloody car?"

I don't know why he was getting so agitated about my saxophone. His life was still in order. But at least I had an opportunity to get back to the future now.

"Fuck me that thing's heavy."

I gave him the science lesson on metal density. He didn't seem very interested or perhaps he didn't understand.

"I need to talk with Guy," I told him and I asked him to help me inside with the sax.

Reluctantly he agreed and we went into the bar. Lorenzo had to assist me and also carry the sax and so Pancho walked along behind.

I shouted feebly across the bar but the music from The Lounge Lizards rendered my voice inaudible and so Lorenzo made the request again. I think they were playing Kissing My Love by Bill Withers and Victoria really had got the groove on the funky rhythm guitar and Ebony Tony was grinding out some mean organ. He had a great voice too. We headed for the back bar where the kitchen door was situated but Guy was standing in the doorway talking with Martina who was leaning at the bar sipping a pint of beer from a frozen glass.

As we approached, Guy let out a high-pitched scream and started shouting, "Get that thing away from me." He was I think referring to the crucifix around Lorenzo's neck. I doubt if he was referring to Pancho as the dog had sat next to him outside, although Pancho had been a little uneasy. Lorenzo was unaware of this and so we moved closer.

There was a slow rise in noise outside until it reached a crescendo and the building started to rattle as a strong wind got up and the ground shook as if there was an earthquake. At the same time there was the loud buzzing of thousands of flies and the room was filled with the smell of burning flesh. Martina knew instinctively what the problem was.

She reached across the bar and picked up the knife that

had been used to slice lemons. Her sword fencing instincts had kicked in and she immediately swung around to cut the crucifix hanging on a leather cord from Lorenzo's neck.

I felt the warm red blood squirt across my face and Lorenzo released his grip on me and fell to the floor gurgling and murmuring "Cazzo". I could do nothing but stand on the spot as I heard him drown on his last breath face down on the floor.

Pancho had seen his master being attacked and so he leapt at Martina's hand grabbing it tightly between his huge lupine teeth. She had fallen forwards plunging the knife deep into Lorenzo's chest as she screamed in agony from the dog bite.

All the accompanying sounds stopped as quickly as they had started and silence filled the air for a brief second. It was then broken by shrieks of grief as Martina fell to the floor realizing what she had done.

The band had stopped and Ebony Tony came to help. He was an Emergency First Responder it turned out, but Lorenzo was dead and there was nothing anyone could do.

"What the fuck have you gone and done you c@@ts," screamed Lager Bob amidst the commotion. "Get a fucking ambulance somebody," he howled at nobody in particular.

An ambulance was patently unnecessary.

22 KISSING MY LOVE

Music: Kissing My Love – Bill Withers

A Soul Father was dead and another was ageing rapidly. #MTn469 came to see if I was unharmed and she took me and sat me down at a vacant table nearby. Pancho walked over and sat down beside me under the table and then flopped down on to the floor. I think he also knew he had had a part to play in the drama and wanted to keep away from the main participants.

I could smell Guy come forwards. He had brought the saxophone and placed it gently on the floor next to me. I heard it touch down softly.

"I think this must be yours. Is it alto or tenor?"

"Tenor," I confirmed.

"You want to talk to me now?" It was more of an order than a request.

#MTn469 came and told me that I was covered in blood. Ignoring Guy she took me off into the ladies toilet to wash my face and beard and to wipe the blood from my waistcoat and sunglasses. She pressed the crucifix she had picked up off the floor into my hand and had trouble speaking because of her grief for Lorenzo even though she had only known him briefly. I slipped the item into my waistcoat pocket and hadn't much to say either.

"Listen darling," I said, "I think there is a way for us to get back to the future. To get out of this mess. What do you think?"

"Lets do it. I hate this place. Our lives were much better back on Campus," she replied.

"Well what do you think?" said the smelly voice the owner of which had remained seated. No ambulance had been called and the Police were not in evidence at the scene of the crime. I sat back down in the chair again.

What I thought was this. We both needed to get back to the future and hopefully our problems would be over as regarding the ageing process. But this was by no means guaranteed. We could use Guy to help us or we could wait for Prof. #ELv15 and Cardinal #BLi55 to assist us. But Guy was here now.

My impatience and fear got the better of me.

"You want this saxophone?"

Guy confirmed his desire to possess the gold saxophone.

"Are there any other catches?"

"Yes I don't want you to return."

This was a difficult one because I had been hoping to play the benefit concert. But now that Lorenzo was dead the whole project was dead with him and I would surely be dead soon or definitely incapable of playing.

"What about the police?" I asked him.

"What about them?" he responded innocently.

I guess there was not much point pursuing that one.

"Here," I said as I slid the sax across the floor to him.

"You want this dog too?"

"No thanks." was the curt reply. I asked #MTn469 to give Pancho to Lager Bob and to ask him to look after him for us.

Lager Bob came over and told us that I was no longer under contract. I told him I didn't mind. He was quite taken by Pancho even though dogs were not allowed in the bar.

Guy escorted me and #MTn469 to the black Mercedes and opened the door for us. She helped me get inside and then slid in next to me on the back seat. I wasn't sure what to expect but then what choice did I have?

"Where are we going?" asked #MTn469.

"We will go back to Güímar. It's where he came through in the portal. I can find it."

She informed Guy that the portals had all been closed. She did this in a sort of hoity toity voice that I'd never heard her use before. Maybe she'd had another ageing fit herself?

He dismissed her remark casually.

After that, the conversation stopped and the journey proceeded in silence and because I was blind I had no way of knowing where he was taking us and I was asleep for most of the journey.

I woke up to find #MTn469 standing outside the car waking me up with Guy standing nearby. She had a strange almost guilty tone to her voice.

Honestly we could have been anywhere and #MTn469 wasn't any the wiser.

"Follow me," he said, and we followed him.

"Where are we?" I whispered to #MTn469 but I'm sure Guy heard.

"We are at the base of what seems to me to be a large pyramid with a flat top," she answered.

I was as satisfied as I could be and so we moved forward.

"Make sure I never see you again," ordered Guy.

   I knew we were through the doors to the future as the noise changed to total silence and then the doors slid closed behind us.

   I leant on the wall and slid onto the floor in exhaustion. #MTn469 sat down beside me and let out a deep sigh.

23 BRIEF RETURN TO THE FUTURE

Music: Summer Breeze – Isley Bros

We both lay locked together on the floor for what felt like an eternity. I felt my strength and vitality slowly returning and when I opened my eyes I saw that my life-partner's beauty had resumed its youthful appearance.

I looked into her adorable clear blue eyes and she looked into mine. I caressed her lips with my own and tasted her tongue. I ran my hands through her soft blond hair and I wondered if all women were exactly the same. I felt the testosterone flow in my blood.

"Guy propositioned me."

"Guy did what?"

"He asked me if I wanted to fuck him."

"When?"

"When you were asleep in the car."

"Fucking bastard. No I don't believe it."

"He did. He said I was the epitome of eternal beauty. Said he wanted to fuck my ass off and asked me to leave you in the future on your own. Said he had the power to reverse rapid ageing. To make me beautiful again."

I knew at that moment I had to go back and wondered if it was possible to save Lorenzo at the same time as having a quiet word with Guy and perhaps stuff the crucifix in my pocket into his smelly mouth and see what happens.

"I'm going back," I said as I slicked my hair back behind my ears and pulled it straight and then grabbed my beard between my fingers and twisted it. I then twisted my hair into a topknot as an afterthought because I had nothing to tie my hair back with.

"Lets go home and make love?" she pleaded.

I couldn't just leave things as they were. I had the power and the ability to change things.

"Later. I've got work to do," and I recalled that Guy didn't want to see me again. But could he prevent me?

I looked at the date and time display on the wall panel. I calculated that it was about two hours ago that Lorenzo had been killed and so I made the adjustment on the controls.

I was about to push the button to open the doors when #MTn469 took my hand gently to stop me. She reminded me about the rapid ageing. I didn't plan to be there so long that it would affect me but of course as she also reminded me; things don't always go according to plan. And in any case it would mean that there was two of me at the one time and space co-ordinates and she didn't know what might happen.

"Can't you go later? Why do you never have time for me?"

It was a question I couldn't answer.

"Perhaps you could find out if there is a solution to the problem of rapid ageing outside of our natural environment? But first close the door behind me and then count to sixty then open the door again to let me back in. OK?"

She reluctantly agreed to do this. I pushed the button to open the door and stepped out. The door slid closed silently behind me and the smell of sulphur made me wretch so hard I doubled up.

The black Mercedes was still sitting there with the engine running and the driver waiting. It was surrounded by a thick swarm of flies.

I fought my way through the black swarm to the car and the window slid down. He told me to get in and so I walked around to the front passenger seat and slipped inside. Fortunately the inside was devoid of insects.

"I knew you wouldn't be long. I thought I told you that I never wanted to see you again?" He laughed he said this and handed me a small mirror with some white powder lined up ready to march on it. I declined. I knew what it was.

"Not much of this about now. Your species is so ingenious. You find the most sophisticated ways to destroy yourselves and pretend that it is fun."

"What happened? Did you do this?" I was shocked at the desolation. The sky was black and the sun barely visible although it was obvious it was daytime. The ground was burned black and the plants were all dead.

"You flatter me, but then you are only human after all. Don't put your blame on me," and he laughed and continued. "I am only a lesser god but I do have some skills. But no, this was mankind's doing."

"In half an hour?"

"I have the ability to warp time and space. Knowing your human mind I was certain that you would return and I wanted to show you the end result of human ingenuity."

I was listening. What else could I do? But I was still counting to sixty in my head. I thought that I'd be safe from rapid ageing if I stayed for one minute.

"I could have destroyed mankind at any time I wanted to. One huge eruption that would have blotted out the sun and suffocated every living thing. But it is only mankind that is the problem; all the other living things did not deserve to die. Humans want their basic human needs which includes things not very basic."

"Spare me the sermon, just tell me what happened." His breath was annoying me and I needed to be rid of him.

"You kill for pleasure. You eat for entertainment. You destroy in order to create illusory benefits. You are slaves to your egos and you are only concerned about one thing, yourselves."

"But you are Satan, so were we made in your image?"

"You have made yourselves into your own image. It's important to note that you see the world around you as a reflection of your own self."

We both sat silently for a moment and then he continued.

"You are not the first to get a glimpse of this. Your Prof. #ELv15 was also privileged to sit with me many years ago."

"He's seen this?" It was incredulous.

"With you?" I said as an afterthought. I was shocked.

"You would do well to learn from him."

"Why him?"

"Rock and Roll of course. It is my music."

"And Soul Music isn't?"

"Ha that is the music of the other side, you know what I mean."

I knew whom he meant. He couldn't bring himself to mention His name and Elvis was a Rock & Roller and that is the Devil's music.

"Is that why there are so many clones of Prof. #ELv15?"

"We need more of him, I just can't get enough."

"And Cardinal #BLi55 too," he confirmed.

I'd discounted Cardinal #BLi55 as a pompous old fool but maybe I was wrong.

"Why him?" I was curious.

"He was or is a rock guitar virtuoso. And he's a one off. Unfortunately he has a tendency to think for himself."

The Cardinal was going up in my estimation.

"Your species always knew that population growth had to come to an end and now it has."

"Everybody gone?" I couldn't believe it but it seemed plausible.

"All except one. You know who she is. She keeps me company."

"Martina?"

He just smiled and sniffed from the mirror and shook his head as if to clear his sinuses.

"And me and #MTn469 and the rest of us, where did we come from?"

"Specially selected. A small group of specimens."

Now I knew or at least guessed why Martina and #MTn469 looked identical and it was very worrying. I felt in my pocket for the crucifix. It was still there. But I decided now was not the time. The damage was done and dispensing with Guy now was too late. It needed to be done earlier in the game.

I had counted to forty-five.

"Now get out of the fucking car and don't let me see you again, there's a good chap."

I walked round the car through the thick swarm of flies and into the open door of the portal without looking back to the dismal scene of destruction.

I heard him shout "she kisses nice."

24 RETURN TO THE FUTURE

Music: Knock On Wood – Eddie Floyd

We felt the room ascend. The doors opened. I guess they had been waiting for us all this time.

"We were expecting you #TMp319."

The voice of Cardinal #BLi55 was as unique as the giant shadow he cast across his poor penitents in the doorway.

"We do not see the saxophone #TMp319, don't tell us you left it behind."

I didn't want to tell him so I didn't.

"You gave it to Guyaota didn't you?"

I acknowledged his assumption as correct with a simple shake of the head.

"Come with me," he ordered silently.

"And you, you get back to your duties," he ordered #MTn469 and added, "You are out of uniform."

We sat in his control chamber. And he explained that Guy or Guyaota was in fact Satan and his ownership of the sax was going to lead to the destruction of mankind or to be correct had already led to it. Once he had learned to play certain notes on it he would be able to create such a huge eruption on El Teide that it would wipe out civilization completely.

"He told me that it was mankind's doing?" I interjected. I guess it sounded like I was pleading Guy's case.

"Do you believe a word he says?"

I wasn't sure that I should answer that question.

"We need you to go back and get the sax."

"OK. But what about rapid ageing?"

"You shouldn't be there long enough for it to be a problem."

"But in case of any eventuality?"

The Cardinal took out a small bottle from his desk drawer it was marked CBD Oil. He held it up in front of my face to read and told me to take three drops on the tip of my tongue. It would be effective for twenty-four hours.

Prof. #ELv15 came into the chamber and sat down. This was the first time I'd seen him without his costume and wig. He was wearing spectacles and his strawberry blond hair was swept back. He looked identical to Lager Bob.

"What you lookin' at you c@@t," he challenged telepathically.

"Sorry but I've never seen you out of costume before," I thought back.

"Button it son. What have you done to your hair? You look like a c@@t with that man bun thing on your head, you fucking nonce."

I decided to steer the silent telepathic conversation on another course. "CBD. What does that mean?"

"Can Beat Death," answered Cardinal #BLi55.

"Really," I said with a giggle.

"Listen son what the fuck is so funny?"

"Nothing," I answered trying to suppress my laugh.

"You need to go back and get the sax. We will set the co-ordinates for you to a little bit before you gave Guyaota the sax. Just bring it back. And remember everything in the past isn't guaranteed to be the same as before. There will be subtle differences. So just be aware of that."

The Cardinal then explained that although I'd been in the past I shouldn't anticipate it to be exactly the same because there was only one of me at that event the last time and now there would be two of me and so it had to be different. I sort of understood and so I discovered even revisiting the past has no certainty to it.

"What about the trial for the killing of the deputy?"

"We can talk about that when you get back. We will look favourably on your good behaviour."

"How will I get back from the past?"

"One of us will come and get you," confirmed Cardinal #BLi55.

"Meet me back here in thirty minutes. Now go and get a shave and a haircut and get back into uniform," ordered Cardinal #BLi55.

I went back to my quarters and #MTn469 was there to meet me with her hair of gold and lips like cherries. I asked her to crop my hair and remove my beard and I told her I was going back officially to recover the sax.

I also told her about CBD Oil and she handed me a capsule.

"Take this when you are back in the past. Your immune system will go into suspense and you will not age until you get back here where the Network will automatically reactivate it. It's what Prof. #ELv15 and his band of karaoke stars has been using."

She didn't know what it was or she didn't want to tell me. Either way I still trusted my life-partner and so I put the capsule in the pocket of my leather waistcoat. I had no intention of changing my clothes. These felt more suitable for the important journey I was going to take.

I returned to meet Cardinal #BLi55. He had set the co-ordinates and so I stepped into the portal as he scolded me for not being properly dressed. I just shrugged it off. This time I popped out in the big shopping center near The Duke of Wellington in Playa de Las Americas.

.

25 SECOND COMING

Music: I Feel Good – James Brown

I was very puzzled by the concept that in the past things would not be exactly the same as before and this thought was at the forefront of my mind.

Nobody seemed to notice or seemed to care that I had just popped out of thin air in the middle of a shopping center. People were too busy with their own lives and their shopping to notice.

This newer time portal was different to the ones I had used previously, as it didn't have a door. You just were not in the same place anymore it was just like magic. Inside the portal room one second and then pop, you were there at the time and destination. It would be interesting to see how it worked to get me back again to the future.

I felt much more comfortable with a shaved head and face and I adjusted my hat and sunglasses and I felt good. I'd like to find the Harley Davidson and go for a ride but I had a task to perform. Hopefully, but because there was no guarantee, could I prevent Lorenzo's murder? I suppose if I could do that, retain the sax and if I could remain permanently young, I could stay and perform the benefit concert whenever that might be.

Then I caught a glimpse of somebody that I recognized. It was The Babushka and she was walking a very small dog, a Chihuahua I think. It trotted along rapidly behind her trying to keep up as her long slender legs carried her gracefully through the shopping mall. She was very expensively dressed and dripping with jewelry.

I was curious to find out where she was going and followed her for a few minutes and realized she was heading in the direction of The Duke of Wellington. She hadn't been there on the day of the murder and as far as I was aware she'd never been in the place so maybe this was one of the anomalies I had to look out for.

She went into The Duke of Wellington and I was relieved that it still looked the same and had the same name. If the pub had been called the Emperor Napoleon I would have been well out of my depth.

My plan B was to make sure Lorenzo didn't wear the crucifix or if he did, to make sure he took it off. That way Martina had no need to use the knife and thus the incident could be avoided. My already well thought out plan A was to ram the fucking crucifix into Guy's mouth but I didn't think he would be terribly compliant.

The infestation of flies and the strong wind and shaking of the ground hadn't started yet so I had plenty of time. However my ancient self, together with Lorenzo and Pancho were not outside chatting on the terrace and I went directly inside and headed for the back bar where the kitchen was located.

Guy was not in the doorway and the persons of interest were nowhere to be seen. I remembered that I still had the mobile phone that Lager Bob had given me and so I took it out and rang his number. After a few rings I heard his voice.

"Hello Lager Bob it's me Tom Perignon."

"Hello, hello, who is this please?"

I repeated myself. I shouted louder because the background noise from The Lounge Lizards was deafening.

"Look I don't want any Payment Protection Insurance. Now be a good boy and piss off. I've told you lot before," and he hung up.

Well that was that.

There was a beautiful black girl leaning up against the bar drinking a pint of beer from a frozen glass. She was tall and very slim and she had a big Afro hairstyle and blue eye make-up. She turned and looked at me casually.

"Can I help you," she asked in English with an East African accent.

"I'm looking for Lorenzo?"

The band rendered my voice inaudible I think they were playing Kissing My Love by Bill Withers and Victoria really had got the groove on the funky rhythm guitar and Ivory Tony was grinding out some mean organ. He had a great voice too for a white guy.

"I'm sorry I can't hear you." She shouted back at me.

"Lorenzo."

I screamed a bit louder. I'm not used to talking and so shouting was not in my repertoire.

She shook her head to indicate she didn't understand. I moved closer. But then she realized what I had said and pointed to the front bar. I walked through and saw Lorenzo sitting at a table with Lager Bob and The Babushka.

"What do you want son?" asked Lager Bob as I stood in front of them, It must have appeared confrontational because they all looked a little uneasy.

I could see Lorenzo was not wearing his priestly attire and he didn't recognize me. He was looking very casual in a flowery Hawaiian shirt and jeans. This is why I didn't see him in the bar as I was expecting to see a Soul Father in clerical clothing.

"Lorenzo it's me Tom. Tom Perignon."

Lorenzo looked up and seemed confused as you might expect somebody to be under the circumstances. I took off my hat and sunglasses. Slowly he comprehended what I had said. The small dog that I had seen The Babushka walking with, was now sitting on her lap and it started yapping.

"Quiet Pancho," ordered Lorenzo.

"Pancho?" I was my turn to be confused but then I realised this was just another anomaly.

"Listen Lorenzo I need to talk to you privately."

He got up and we went to the back bar where I introduced myself again and explained that the purpose of my visit was to prevent his murder by Guyaota the Guanche Devil who lives inside the volcano at El Teide. He seemed unconvinced, unbelieving even.

"Listen to me, where is he. Guy I mean?"

Lorenzo just stared at me.

"Guy the chef. Lager Bob's business partner and driver."

Lorenzo just stared at me and said, "Bob's business partner is his wife. There's nobody here called Guy."

"What's the chef called?"

"Rita."

"Rita is Lager Bob's daughter isn't she?" Lorenzo confirmed my remark with a shake of the head.

"And the old guy and his wife. From the future. They had rapid ageing. He had a gold saxophone. Where are they?"

"Are you feeling alright?" As he said this Lorenzo placed his hand upon my arm in a comforting sort of manner.

I felt the presence of somebody standing behind me and turned around. It was my life-partner. I was about to introduce her as #MTn469 but thought the better of it so I put my hand around her shoulders and pulled her close. I whispered in her ear to ask her how she had gotten here and she said she had been sent to help me. Then she told me that she was not #MTn469. She was #MTn477 another clone from the same batch. I hoped she was not as predictable as her predecessor although she probably would be.

"This is my wife," I had to think of a name as calling her by her hash-tag seemed inappropriate. "Martina."

I repeated myself to sound more convincing. "This is my wife Martina." I had to think hard on this as I normally called #MTn469 Josephine in private. By calling her by a different name I hoped any crisis that might arise in my head would be resolved.

"Martina meet Martina," and Lorenzo gestured to the black woman at the bar.

"And the other Martina, the one with the tattoo and the blue hair. Where is she?"

"Other Martina? What other Martina?"

On looking at #MTn477 I realized that I had not taken the capsule her predecessor had given me and so I fumbled in my pocket. There it was, the small capsule nestled beside the crucifix from the previous past that I had placed there in the future. I asked for a glass of water.

"Rita is Lager Bob's secret love child isn't she?"

"I don't know about that. You'd better ask him. But maybe best not in front of his wife, you know. She's sitting over there beside him."

"Ok tell me how do I know that his name is Lager Bob?"

"I don't know. And his name is not Lager Bob it's Vodka Bob."

I hesitated, "It was me who just phoned him."

"Was it?"

I was now getting more than a little frustrated.

"Have you escaped from the lunatic asylum, the one at the penitentiary?" I asked because I needed an anchor stone in my logic.

This was greeted with total silence and Lorenzo just stared at me.

"Martina, this one here was the nurse in the psychiatric ward there?" And I nodded in the direction of black Martina.

"Who are you?" he demanded.

"I'm from an alternative future. We were going to play a benefits concert to fund The Church of Everyday People so that we could provide homes for the minimum-wage hotel workers sleeping on the beach here."

I decided to be more pragmatic and adapt to the current circumstances. I realized at that point I had probably been duped into returning to the past and there was no going back to the future. This was probably some sort of punishment dreamed up by Cardinal #BLi55. I made a mental note to ask #MTn477 why #MTn469 was not here and she was.

"Listen I'm the sax player in the band, I'm your partner your number two."

"Where's your sax?"

This was the bit I couldn't be bothered to explain.

"It got stolen." It was the first thing that came to mind and in the interests of brevity a very appropriate response or so I thought.

"Well we already have a horn section and I'm not sure we need another sax player. Especially one without an instrument."

They didn't need another sax player. I was stunned. This was my project as much as it was his. What the actual fuck?

"Where do you live?" Lorenzo asked me.

I had no answer because I didn't know. I guess the reality of the situation was that I was homeless and so most likely going to be living on the beach with lots of other people and with #MTn477 too. And of course we didn't have jobs and we needed money to survive. We didn't have any documents in order to satisfy any of the formalities that I had learned about in my previous visit.

"We live quite nearby. I'll pop by from time to time and perhaps we can discuss this a bit more." I took the hint and left.

26 LIVING IN THE PAST

Music: Man Does Not Live – Sly & the Family Stone

Now I didn't even have access to the priestly robes so that I could claim charity under the guise of the Poor Fathers of Tenerife. #MTn477 and I had to beg for food and water and we slept on the beach for several weeks until we built up a network of friends and survived on a diet of bananas and tomatoes. Eventually we moved into a vacant cave in La Caleta formerly a small fishing port north of Las Americas and now a small tourist trap. It had only become vacant because the previous inhabitant had burned to death there, as she was unable to escape when her stove erupted in the entrance of the cave.

To survive like this you need to become part of the community and so slowly we were absorbed into the itinerant society of workers who kept the tourist economy thriving in Tenerife but who couldn't afford to live there.

It was now late October and we were grateful for the shelter that the cave afforded because it was quite chilly at night and it rained occasionally. There was a great view of the sky and I loved to watch all the 'planes arrive especially at night when you could see the aircraft lights at a distance as they turned over the north west of the island and made their approach. I wondered where they came from and where they went back to. I thought about all the people travelling here and wondered what their lives and families were like. I guess they had children or were themselves children of other people, children of other children.

I went back to The Duke of Wellington several times in the hope of meeting with Lorenzo but I never saw him although Lager Bob or more correctly Vodka Bob was present. But he didn't have the same warmth towards me as he had in my previous experiences and so I decided not to talk with him. This ruled out any opportunity to borrow the Fat Boy assuming he had access to one in this epoch.

I had found myself a job in a finca not too far from our cave, where I could utilize my knowledge of hydroponics and where I seem to have created a masterpiece of engineering and art and which was becoming a local tourist attraction. I had built a water feature that was powered by a non-stop Herons fountain. I needed it to aerate water for the hydroponics garden and I refused to power that with electricity. Actually I had no choice because we didn't have electricity in our cave and nobody else did either. I had built a prototype first and it was situated near the mouth of our cave where we could enjoy listening to the sounds of the water cascade from three giant bowls. It was building this prototype that had got me the job at the finca. Normally a Herons fountain does not demonstrate perpetual motion; it will eventually come to a stop. However with an obvious subtle adjustment to the original concept it will run forever.

One morning as I was going to work I met Lorenzo walking Pancho the Chihuahua along the beach. We arranged to meet at The Duke of Wellington to discuss the cryptocurrency project. This and The Church of Everyday People was something he knew nothing about and so I outlined it all again for him. He seemed quite interested.

It just so happened that Lorenzo had a gig playing at the

finca later that day as he often performed a solo set in various places with his guitar. He said he might be able to get me a loan of an alto saxophone and bring it with him. I wasn't sure about playing music because I had dismissed the idea in favour of hydroponics engineering. Being a performer was just an exercise in vanity and now growing food efficiently had become my life's passion. It also helped me to survive whereas music would never achieve that. Also I don't suit the alto sax. It's too small and I am very tall so it looks a bit silly. The tenor better matches my physique and better suits the music I like to play.

I had also come to know that the only reason people are doing most of the things they do in this life is because they have to. I had a worry-free existence in the future but here in the Twenty First Century I had responsibilities such as finding food and accommodation. Fortunately because we were cloned to be sterile, the prospect of being responsible for children of my own was not something I needed to worry about. But for some reason I felt concerned about other peoples' offspring.

I encountered a lot of children in my work at the finca as the primary hydroponics engineer because it was a sort of commune where people went to hang out with their families. Actually there were a lot of families and they spent a lot of time together. This was something #MTn477 and I were unfamiliar with.

I think not being able to have children was a particular issue for her although it was a subject that I had never encountered with #MTn469. #MTn477 never wanted to talk about this subject. Actually she never wanted to talk about anything because she was never at home and she seemed to have amassed a circle of friends, all of them male. I wasn't surprised because she was a stunning looking woman and I wasn't jealous because she was not my life-partner. That role went to #MTn469. But it does get very frustrating when the woman you are sharing a cave with returns home regularly at five in the morning totally the worse for drink. I was learning that #MTn477 was a woman who always put her own needs first and I'm guessing that #MTn469 would have reacted the same way in the same circumstances so I have to be thankful that my love #MTn469 was not the one put to the test.

#MTn477 was also an expert tennis player something she had learned in the simulator and so she spent most of her time burning off the calories and keeping herself trim by playing against Martina. The only time she would let me play with her was in a game of doubles when we both played against Lorenzo and Martina. I think there was quite a lot of competition in our relationship and I think this is the reason why simulations were used in our future world. It was in order to reduce conflict caused by human nature and the desire to be superior to another.

There was quite a lot of tension in Lorenzo and Martina's blossoming relationship too because they both worked in time-share sales for competing companies. One of the reasons Bob and Lorenzo were offhand with me when I first met them this time round was that they thought I'd come to get my deposit back from a cancelled time-share contract. They had a policy of non-refunds.

In the previous discussions about cryptocurrency it had been proposed that it would be asset-backed by tantalite obtained from coltan. This material would be damaging to the planet as it needed to be mined and so I felt it unsuitable for the project. My desire was to asset-back the crypto with hydroponically grown produce and hydroponics systems. The set-up costs for a commercial hydroponics farm are quite large and so any ICO should fund that. It was still very much an idea of my own but I was happy to share it.

Lorenzo had talked me into playing some numbers with him because it was Halloween, which is a very important festival in the Hispanic world as it celebrates death.

Death is something we don't have to concern ourselves too much with in the future. We are engineered to live a set amount of time and then we expire on a given date, our expiry date. Death does not come as a surprise. It is a certainty, unless we meet premature expiry due to accident. Disease has been eradicated and so there are no concerns about that.

Grief is also something that we didn't encounter but instinctively I knew I was suffering from it. This was because I had been very close to #MTn469 and although #MTn477 was identical we did not have the same shared experiences. I missed #MTn469 because she was my soul mate and #MTn477 could never replace her. I guess this was behind the friction in our relationship. And of course #MTn477 was out of her comfort zone too and away from her life-partner #TMp201 a slightly earlier variant of me.

Lorenzo told me we needed to dress up for the Halloween party and so we decided to go to the fancy dress store but as we had no money we would need to steal something, a skill I had acquired out of necessity. Unfortunately all the stuff they had was too small for me. I recalled that in the previous existence Lorenzo had worked in the laundry at the penitentiary and so I asked him if there was a laundry nearby. There was, but we were unable to liberate two priestly robes freshly laundered or otherwise. I explained my idea about The Soul Fathers. This was something else he was unfamiliar with but he warmed to the idea.

#MTn477 can be a real pain at times, most of the time to be honest, but sometimes she comes in useful. After my early shift at the finca, I went home for my siesta and was pleasantly surprised to find that she had a present for me. Nearby is a nudist beach and on her early morning swim she had found a pile of clothes. Buying new clothes is out of the question for us because we have limited funds and so she brought them home to the cave. The clothes were two set of priests' robes and two sets of nuns' robes including crucifixes. She was adamant that there had been nobody else in the sea and that the clothes had been abandoned. Perhaps two pairs of religious romantics had absconded. I hoped to not be hunted down by nude nuns and stark naked sacerdotes and then accosted for the return of their attire.

In the evening we both got ready for the fancy dress party,

me as a priest and #MTn477 as a nun. On the way to the finca I found a lookie-lookie man and gave him confession in exchange for a hat and sunglasses for Lorenzo. And so the roles were reversed from our previous encounter.

At the finca I persuaded Lorenzo to dress up and in return I played some numbers on the alto he had brought, and so The Soul Fathers were reborn.

After we had played we sat down to have a good discussion about using an asset-backed cryptocurrency to fund a project. He warmed to the idea of The Church of Everyday People. He himself was living in a twenty-year-old Ford Escort and he sympathized with the homeless minimum-wage workers as his time-share sales skills needed to be worked on a little.

We agreed that we would join forces and the project was reborn if that is the proper terminology.

Actually we went down so well as The Soul Fathers that we decided to play as a duo around the bars in the area and make some money in the evenings as it carried less risk than shoplifting. There was some small risk though because the local police sent employment inspectors round to make sure that poor minimum-wage homeless performers were paying the proper taxes on their meager earnings.

It struck me as unfair that we should have to pay taxes and get nothing in return but this seems to be the way with Twenty First Century slavery. I had no papers and so could get no benefits from the government of the people by the people. But fortunately we only worked in places where we were paid in cash but unfortunately those were the ones that the police targeted and eventually closed down for paperwork anomalies.

27 THE BENEFIT GIG

Music: Living In America – James Brown

The festive season came and went and Lorenzo and I went from strength to strength as performers. We were double booked for a gig on New Year's Eve and somebody said that we couldn't be in two places at once. I wondered if this wasn't strictly true. Given that I had now travelled to an alternative past to the one I had been in previously, it might actually be possible to be in many places at once.

As before, the community of Neil Diamond karaoke artists was displaced from their gigs in favour of The Soul Fathers. But due to the local government and police more and more venues were being closed down. It was as if the government of the island wanted fewer tourists to come or maybe wanted tourists to come but to not enjoy themselves. It was hard to tell.

Bob took an interest in our relative success and warmed to the idea of The Church of Everyday People asset-backed by a version of hydroponics where the nutrients for the plants are derived from fish waste. It's known as aquaponics. This is considered superior to hydroponics because it is classed as Organic whereas standard hydroponics is not. Every green plant needs the same ingredients to grow and this can be supplied in a number of ways. Additionally with aquaponics there is also profit from the sale of fish. As a vegetarian I was not keen on this but Bob and his business team of his wife The Babushka and his daughter Rita were more commercially minded and so I agreed to this subtle modification of the business idea.

In order to kick start the project they agreed to organize a benefit concert featuring The Lounge Lizards but Lorenzo and I had a more well-developed plan and so The Soul Fathers benefit gig was reborn and we incorporated Martina and #MTn477 as dancers dressed as nuns so that they didn't feel left out.

The concert was planned for Easter Monday, which gave us almost four months of rehearsals. Meanwhile life went on as usual and we continued to perform as a duo in bars and live our respective private lives in caves and in clapped out vehicles.

The local Hell's Angels were engaged as security and as event managers and consequently the gig was held in a motorcycle repair center's car park on the south of the island. I was quite surprised at how small the venue was and that the crowd capacity was not large. But Rita had managed to get a TV sponsorship deal from a Belgian company that would boost the profits. She had also acquired a nun's clothing so that she could dance on stage with us. I hoped she didn't want to sing though.

As a consequence I got to spend a lot of time with Rita and she had earned my respect and trust, something that #MTn477 had failed miserably to achieve. Rita is a few years older than me but she looked good for whatever age she was because although she's stunningly attractive her real beauty comes from within. And with a personality like that, looks are unimportant although it's definitely a bonus. I was not surprised to discover that she had become a grandmother at a very young age because she had also been a mum at a very young age. The reason I was not surprised is because she is a person who has learned to put the needs of another before her own. This is another example of necessity forcing people to reach higher and become better. It's something that has been massaged out of my society in the future because the state has taken control of everything. I was glad she was not fitted with a dropDead@33.gene.

I was quite surprised to find out that she felt the same about me as I did about her and so Rita and I spent a very special night together. Her pragmatic logic advised me not to give too much concern to #MTn477's behaviour because we didn't have any children together and she was not my life-partner. For all intents and purposes we were only sharing a cave and an altered past together. Also #MTn477 only had the emotional maturity of a three-year-old girl and this wasn't her fault because she had been taken from her natural environment.

Rita also shared my views that mutual respect was a fundamental part of any successful relationship. Rita was my soul mate.

I couldn't explain to her about my previous visit to the past or my reasons for visiting this past. She would just have thought I was crazy. But I prodded the subject tenderly and discussed Guyaota the Devil of the Guanches who was imprisoned inside El Teide. All she would say was "The Devil comes to you disguised as everything you have ever desired."

Predictably the police and the local government intervened to try to stop the benefit concert. But Bob is a smart cookie and the restrictions they referred to applied to venues where the audience was more than two hundred people. However Bob was only going to sell one hundred and ninety-nine tickets. Of course this was all Rita's thinking.

The day of the event came and when we got to the gig there were hundreds of Guardia Civil blocking the entrance. There were also about one hundred and fifty Hell's Angels blocking the entrance from the inside. Fortunately the band were all there including the Jet Free Horns proudly wearing their red work shirts.

They had all made their way earlier on a Jet Free company coach that they had borrowed.

    We had come in Bob's black Mercedes 500 driven by Rita and Bob had wisely brought along the town mayor who had already given us written authority. We all remonstrated with the head of the Guardia Civil. Unlike the local police they do not answer to the local mayor.

    As Bob and the mayor were arguing with the captain of the Guardia Civil I told Lorenzo and the three girls to come with me. We strolled casually over to the Guardia Civil helicopter parked on some land just off the roadway. It was unmanned; I guess the crew was off having a cheeky smoke. Lorenzo guessed what I was about to do but didn't believe that I could fly the thing. #MTn477 put him right and that she could also fly it too.

    We got in and I primed the engine and started it up. We got off the ground before the crew could stop us.

"You fancy a sightseeing trip first?" I asked. Of course they did and I handed the controls to #MTn477.

    After circling El Teide we headed back to the gig before they could scramble a jet fighter to intercept us. The only way that the Guardia Civil could retain their big cojones was by a display of military authority supported by the air force. I was hoping that they didn't want that televised but I wasn't taking any chances either.

    #MTn477 hovered the helicopter over the big car park. The capo of the Hell's Angels guessed what we were doing although he probably thought it was the Guardia Civil inside the chopper. The crowd moved back and there was enough room to land. The four of us got out and went on stage to join the rest of the band.

    #MTn477 parked the helicopter safely where we had taken it from and nobody was prepared to challenge a nun who had just landed a Guardia Civil chopper perfectly. At the same time the authorities retreated in defeat and allowed the now huge crowd to enter the festival. Nobody checked tickets and there must have been hundreds more people than we had planned for.

As we opened the show with 'Living in America' the James Brown number, I could see at the front of the audience a crowd of ten Elvis Presley tribute singers, all but one dressed identically. I knew whom they were and clearly they were still keeping an eye on me.

28 LEAVING TENERIFE IN A HURRY

Music: Hip Hug Her – Booker T & the MG's

The jet taxied in an orderly fashion to the holding point ready for take-off.

"I bet you can fly one of these too?" Lorenzo asked.

I nodded silently signifying that I could.

We had left Bob to organize The Hard Knock Hotel and the Church of Everyday People funded by an asset-backed cryptocurrency.

We were now released from any obligations and we fully intended to remain unobligated. The flight was headed for Brussels where I had another project planned.

All possible charges had been dropped by the Guardia Civil because of the publicity surrounding the charitable work that the benefit concert was going to support.

We relaxed in our seats, the two girls, one black and one white, dressed as nuns on one side of the aisle and myself and Lorenzo sitting together on the other side in our clerical attire.

The engines screamed releasing power for take-off and the Boeing 737 accelerated along the runway and climbed towards the sun. The aircraft banked to the left to turn northwards towards Europe and Lorenzo started to laugh as he looked out of the window.

I leant over him to see what was so funny and could see pillars of smoke rising up from two of the airport buildings down below. I couldn't help myself from laughing either and the girls asked us what was so funny.

Martina didn't know about Lorenzo's past as an arsonist opera singer but I had told Rita all about it and she also let out a little giggle and said, "You men are all the same."

THE END – for now

Printed in Poland
by Amazon Fulfillment
Poland Sp. z o.o., Wrocław